I've Got an Idea

Eric Walters

I'VE GOT AN IDEA

HarperTrophyCanada™
An imprint of HarperCollinsPublishersLtd

I've Got an Idea
© 2004 by Eric Walters. All rights reserved.

Published by HarperTrophyCanada™, an imprint of HarperCollins
Publishers Ltd

HarperTrophyCanada™ is a trademark of HarperCollins Publishers

First published by HarperTrophyCanada™: 2004
This mass market paperback edition: 2006

HarperCollins books may be purchased for educational, business, or sales promotional use through our Special Markets Department.

HarperCollins Publishers Ltd
2 Bloor Street East, 20th Floor
Toronto, Ontario, Canada
M4W 1A8

www.harpercollins.ca

Library and Archives Canada Cataloguing in Publication

Walters, Eric, 1957-
I've got an idea / Eric Walters.

ISBN-13: 978-0-00-639526-3
ISBN-10: 0-00-639526-0

I. Title.
PS8595.A598I93 2006   jC813'.54   C2005-905610-X

OPM 9 8 7 6 5 4 3 2 1

Printed and bound in the United States

For Leon, Mary, and their family—
for helping to bring New York, the city that never
sleeps, alive for me

Chapter One

I heard the classroom door open and glanced up from my work. Mr. Roberts, our vice-principal, entered the room. He was the last person in the world I wanted to see. Just as I was about to get back to work, afraid that he might think I was goofing off and get angry at me again, I spotted the girl trailing behind him. I knew everybody in the school— heck, practically everybody in the whole town—and I definitely had never seen her before. I was positive because she was the sort of person I wouldn't forget.

She had brilliant red hair, cut short, swooped back and buzz-cut around the sides to reveal six or seven studs in each ear. She had lipstick on and dark stuff around her eyes to make them stand out, and her clothes were cool. She didn't look like a sixth-grader— at least not like any sixth-grader in *this* school. More like an extra in a rock video.

Mr. Roberts walked toward Mrs. Ready, who was seated at her desk, and the girl followed behind him. Mr. Roberts leaned over the desk and turned his back to us so he could talk without any of us hearing. The girl looked around the room—she seemed calm and cool. That was the opposite of how I'd be feeling if I were the new kid in the class. Especially if I were starting late, three weeks into the year. We locked eyes. She smiled slightly and I looked away. My cheeks got hot. I knew I was probably blushing, although I hoped she couldn't see it from where she stood.

Almost everybody had stopped even pretending to work and was checking the new kid out. The lone exception was Sam, my best friend. Although he was seated in the very front row, closest to the teacher's desk, he was paying no attention to anything around him. On the floor beside him sat his math book. It had taken him all of two minutes to finish the problems the rest of us had been struggling and sweating over for the last half hour.

Sam was writing away feverishly in his *idea book*— that's what Sam called it. It was a beaten-up old spiral notebook that he carried with him everywhere. He was always making notes: things he wanted to do, plans, drawings. As far as I was concerned, he should have called it his *bad* idea book, because whenever we got in trouble it almost always started with some words scrawled between those covers. When he was working on an idea, he'd hardly notice a fire drill.

Sam and I had been best friends since kindergarten. Even from the beginning I'd always known there was something seriously different about him. It wasn't until a couple of years later, after he'd annoyed and frustrated and generally driven our teachers crazy, that they decided *how* Sam was different. Turned out he was a genius.

At first I didn't really understand what that meant. It wasn't just that he was smarter, or had more information stuffed in his head, or did his work faster than the rest of us—although all of those things were true. What made him a genius was that he saw the world his own way. Sometimes seeing things differently meant he could solve the most complicated problems instantly. Other times the simplest things baffled him. Things like why he had to stay at his desk when he'd finished his work, or why he was wearing a running shoe on one foot and a dress shoe on the other, or where exactly he'd left his lunch and backpack. If I had a dollar for every time I shared my lunch with him when he forgot his, I'd be the richest eleven-year-old in Farmingdale, maybe the whole state of New Jersey.

Sam continued to write away. I was curious to know what he was working on this time. I figured I wouldn't have to wait long. At lunch I'd hear all about it, whether I wanted to or not. Ninety-nine percent of the time, his ideas were either harmless or about something I couldn't even hope to understand. It was the other one percent I'd learned to fear. Those were the ideas that sounded innocent enough but always ended up getting us in trouble.

"I'd like your attention. Could you please put down your pens," Mrs. Ready said.

This was a particularly easy command to obey since—with the exception of Sam—we weren't really giving our pens a workout. Besides, there was a list of classroom rules up on the blackboard, and rule number one was "Listen to Your Teacher" underlined three times. Sam scratched away diligently, oblivious to her words.

"Boys and girls, I would like to introduce the newest member of our class. This is Twilight Stevens."

Muttering could be heard throughout the room, some kids giggled and a couple made faces. "What kind of a name is Twilight?" I heard somebody say, loud enough for the whole class to hear.

Mrs. Ready raised one hand in the air, her signal for us to stop talking, and the noise level dropped off to nothing. We'd all learned it was better for her to raise her hand than to raise her voice. She had a shriek that could shake the walls.

"Twilight, you can be seated at the empty desk near

the back. When you're feeling more comfortable, perhaps tomorrow or the next day, you can tell the class a bit about yourself."

"I'm feeling comfortable right now," Twilight replied.

"Well . . . in that case, umm . . . please proceed," Mrs. Ready said. She sounded surprised.

Twilight stepped over a few feet to the very center of the front of the room. She moved with an air of total confidence.

"Good morning. As Mrs. Ready said, my name is Twilight. Twilight Stevens. Some of you may find my name unusual, but I think it is a wonderful name. I would find it terribly boring to have a run-of-the-mill name . . . one of those you have to share with two or three other people wherever you go."

We had three Ashleys and four Michaels in our class.

"My parents named me Twilight because I was born at the exact moment when the day meets the night. I was born in New York City, although I've lived in cities around the world. My mother is a sculptor and my father is an actor. You might have heard of him—his name is Brice McKinnon."

There was a sudden murmuring in the room: "Brice McKinnon? The *real* Brice McKinnon?"

Twilight's expression changed ever so slightly. A sly smile formed on her lips. She paused. I had no idea who Brice McKinnon was, but I was sure curious to find out.

"Yes," Twilight replied in a quiet voice.

A few of the girls squealed in delight. The rest of the class, including me, just looked confused.

"Twilight," Mrs. Ready asked as she raised her hand again for silence, "I may be a little out of touch, but should I know who your father is?"

"You don't know who Brice McKinnon is, Mrs. Ready?" asked Cindy in total disbelief. "He plays Rex Ryan on *These Days Are Forever*. He's a major hunk!"

Cindy, who knew practically nothing about math, knew everything there was to know about daytime TV. She taped the soaps and watched them every night. I knew because she was always talking about the characters as though they lived in our neighborhood.

"Actually," interrupted Twilight, "if you ask my mother she'll say he's more like major junk than a major hunk. She tossed him out a few months ago."

The class was thrown into silence by this statement, although if I'd listened closely enough I'll bet I could have heard the air escaping out of Cindy as she deflated. She'd just lost out on the chance to meet a soap opera star. A "hunky" one.

"When they separated, my mother said she was tired of living in New York. She said the city was like a gigantic bowl of cereal, filled with nuts and flakes and things she didn't like. That's why she made us move to Farmingdale, so we could be around what she calls 'real people.'"

Chapter Two

The recess bell sounded. All the kids stayed in their seats waiting for Mrs. Ready's permission to leave. Twilight remained standing.

"Perhaps you can tell us as bit more after recess, Twilight. Class dismissed," Mrs. Ready said.

Chair legs scraped against the floor as people got to their feet. Conversations started up as kids moved toward the door. Cindy and a couple of the other girls caught up with Twilight. They started talking and left the class together.

I walked over to Sam. His full attention was focused on his book. When I looked down I could see that he was writing little mathematical formulas beside a diagram. A quick glance confirmed that I had no idea what he was doing, and if I stood there and studied it for the rest of the day, I probably still wouldn't be able to make any sense of it. I just hoped it didn't involve me in any way I'd regret.

Most of the kids had already filed out, and the room was almost quiet.

"Sam, come on, it's recess."

"What?"

"Recess. It's time for recess, come on."

"Just a minute, I have to figure out one more thing, and—"

"Not just a minute!" Mrs. Ready said loudly. "Samuel, go outside. Maybe you don't need a break, but I certainly do. Go!"

Sam sighed and put down his pencil. Lots of things didn't make sense to Sam, particularly when it came to people, but he understood Mrs. Ready really well. She didn't care if Sam was a genius, a general or the president of the United States. You did what she told you to, or else. Both of my parents, who'd gone to Farmingdale P.S. when they were kids, had been in her sixth-grade class. They said she was the same way back then—and when I looked at their class picture, I was shocked to see that she even *looked* the same way back then. The woman had to be at least two hundred years old, and she'd had the same hairstyle for the past thirty!

That was the year my parents first met. My mother

was the new kid who'd moved in that summer. How strange, to meet your future wife in Grade 6!

Sam and I walked through the emptying halls and out into the schoolyard. I guided him through the sea of moving bodies. Sam was trying to explain his newest idea to me, but I was too busy trying to see where Twilight had gone. I stopped when Sam and I were standing on the very edge of the playground, safe from all the people running and roughhousing and tossing balls around.

Sam and I never played at recess. Neither one of us was what you could call good at sports. To be honest, it would be pushing it to say we were just bad; we were the worst. I had a better chance of catching a ball with my face than with my hand. And that really didn't seem fair, since I had two hands and only one face. It bothered me that I was so spazzy. I didn't like to admit it even to myself, but I did want to play sometimes. I had fantasies where I'd be the hero, the one who hit the home run or caught the winning touchdown.

None of this bothered Sam. He didn't see the point in sports. He'd never play unless he was forced to, like in gym class. It was guaranteed we'd always be the last two picked when they made up teams, one of us on either side.

Sam kept going on about his newest idea. I caught little snippets of information—enough to realize it had something to do with whales and pollution—but I wasn't paying enough attention to know any more. I was focused on the far side of the schoolyard, where Twilight was standing with a group of girls. She was facing away from us. I watched her while Sam continued to talk. I nodded my head in agreement and occasionally said "yeah" or "right," and he didn't notice I wasn't really listening.

I wondered what they were talking about over there. I would have paid money to be there, listening, rather than across the yard, *pretending* to listen.

Twilight and the entire group of girls she was with turned and started looking around. I kept watching. Suddenly one of the twins—I couldn't tell from this distance whether it was Kellie or Erin—pointed right at me. My eyes widened in shock and I felt as though I'd been caught doing something bad. I had to fight the urge to look away and pretend I hadn't been watching them, but my attention was riveted on Twilight, who'd broken away from the group and was walking directly toward us. I swallowed hard.

She was coming closer and closer. Maybe she was headed someplace else. I turned around to see where else she could be looking or going. There was nothing but a hawthorn bush and the water tower behind me. I looked back at Twilight. She continued to glide across the pavement.

Sam, of course, hadn't noticed anything. He just talked on and on. I wasn't sure what "echolocation" was, but Sam was talking about it at full speed.

Twilight flashed a smile and gave me a wave. I gave her a little half wave back.

"Hi, guys," she said, stopping right in front of us. "Which one of you is Sam and which one is Alex?"

I was nothing short of shocked. How did she know our names, and what did she want? Surprisingly, Sam stopped talking and looked at her as well.

"I'm Alex . . . and, um . . . this is Sam," I stated apprehensively. I felt my cheeks get hot. Now I *knew* I was blushing.

"I guess you two already know who I am. I had Kellie—or was it Erin—point you two out to me. How do you tell those two apart?" Twilight asked.

"Their hair. Kelly has bangs, Erin has a forehead . . . I mean, they both have foreheads, it's just that Erin wears her hair so that you can see hers, and—"

"Okay, okay, I think I understand."

Twilight gazed at us, looking a bit confused—or was it amused? She cocked her head to one side and stroked her chin. She checked us over from head to toe, and I felt like a bug under a microscope. "Neither of you look very dangerous to me."

"Dangerous! What makes you think we're dangerous?" I asked in alarm.

"I heard you're the two most dangerous guys in the whole school," she answered.

"We're not dangerous. Did Cindy tell you that? She's always making fun of us in one way or—"

"It wasn't Cindy who told me you were dangerous."

Sam started chuckling to himself. We'd been called a lot of things over the years; dangerous wasn't one of them. But it sure had a nicer ring than "brainer" or "brainiac" or "geekoid," names we were usually called. After all, Sam was the genius, and I got better marks than anybody else in the school. Actually, I got better marks than Sam most of the time because, unlike him, I always did my homework and handed in assignments. Sam didn't always bother with details like that.

"You shouldn't be so modest, Alex. It's pretty cool to be known as dangerous," Twilight continued.

"We're not, and whoever told you we are is either stupid or a liar!" I declared firmly.

"Are you calling your vice-principal, Mr. Roberts, stupid or a liar?"

"No, of course I'm not."

"Because if you are, I'm going to have to go and tell him you're spreading rumors about him being a stupid liar. He didn't strike me as the sort of guy who would have a sense of humor about being called names. I'll just go and find him right now." She turned to walk away.

"No!" I shouted.

Twilight turned back around. A few kids playing nearby stopped and turned around as well.

"No," I started again, this time quietly, "I'm not saying Mr. Roberts is a stupid liar. I'm just saying we're not dangerous."

"Make up your mind, Alex, you can't have it both ways. Either you're dangerous or Mr. Roberts is a liar."

"Are you telling me Mr. Roberts told you we're dangerous?" I asked.

"He didn't tell *me* that you were dangerous. But I heard him."

"Yeah, dangerous. I like that. Me and Alex . . . two dangerous dudes," Sam crowed.

"Knock it off, Sam," I said sharply.

"Okay, Alex, if you say so. After all, I wouldn't want to get a dangerous dude like you mad at me."

Twilight giggled. I felt a small stabbing pain in my head, right behind my right ear. I had read how that could be the first sign of a brain tumor or a cerebral bleed. I wondered if all the stress of this had caused me to pop a blood vessel. At the very least I knew I'd fried some brain cells. I reached a hand up and started massaging the side of my head.

"So, would you like to know who he told that you two were dangerous?" she asked.

Part of me wanted her to just leave me alone and go away. The other part needed to know. Besides, there was something weird about having her here. There was a strange sort of fuzzy feeling in the back of my head that was competing with the stabbing pain. I'd never felt anything like it before. Maybe it was a warning sign my brain *was* frying.

"Please, could you explain it?" I asked.

Twilight smiled. I knew she was enjoying my confusion. "He told my mother about you two when she was registering me this morning."

"And then your mother told you, right?"

"No, of course not. She wouldn't repeat gossip. She always says big people talk about ideas and little people talk about other people."

"Then, how could you . . . ?" I let the sentence trail off.

"It's simple. After my mother and I met with Mr. Roberts in his office, she asked if I would leave so they could discuss something in private. They made me wait outside by the secretary's desk. That's when I heard."

"You couldn't hear them talking from there, even if they left the door open," I noted. "I know from experience."

"I bet you've had *plenty* of experience being in the office," she said, laughing. "But believe me, you can hear everything that's said in Mr. Roberts' office. All you have to do is turn on the intercom."

My jaw dropped.

"Come on, Alex, don't look so shocked. I bet you would have done the same thing if you'd thought of it."

"No!" I answered quickly. "No way would I ever do that!"

"I would have, in a second. What a great idea!" Sam said enthusiastically.

"Thank you. I thought it was pretty clever," Twilight responded proudly. "Although, to tell you the truth, I almost didn't. I was afraid the secretary might come back in. She is one scary-looking lady. Then I figured, what could she do, kill me?"

Twilight was right. Mrs. Watson, our school secretary, had never killed anybody. She'd *threatened* to kill kids, but she'd never actually taken a life.

"It only seemed fair. After all, they were talking about *me* in there, so I thought it was right to listen in. I was pretty sure what my mother wanted to talk about anyway."

"What?" I asked.

"She wanted to know if the school could handle me."

"What do you mean, *handle* you?" I stepped slightly back, as if she might bite or infect me with germs.

"I've been in a few private schools before and I've been . . . asked to leave."

"You mean suspended?" Sam asked.

"No, not suspended. Expelled. My mother explained some of the things I've done that got me into trouble, and Mr. Roberts told her they had experience dealing with children with similar kinds of behavior. That's when he mentioned the two of you."

"He mentioned us?" Sam asked innocently. "That was nice."

My stomach started bubbling away. Great, I was going to get a stomachache to complement the pain in my head.

"I hate to break your bubble, Sammy, but I don't think 'nice' had anything to do with it," Twilight chirped.

The recess bell rang loudly. Kids all around stopped playing and started assembling in lines to go back into the school.

"We'd better get in line," I said.

"That's cool. I'd like to hear what you two did that got you in trouble. You can tell me at lunch," Twilight said.

"Lunch?" I questioned.

"Yes, lunch. That's what we call it in New York when people put food in their mouths around noon. You people do have lunch around here, don't you?" she asked sarcastically.

"Of course we have lunch!"

"Good. Then we have a date," she replied. She flashed me a quick smile and then turned and walked away to line up before I even had a chance to reply. Sam and I started to walk after her.

"Dangerous . . . I like that," Sam said quietly.

I grabbed him by the shoulder and spun him toward me. "Don't you go starting! You know as well as I do that we're not dangerous. We're the two least dangerous people I know, so just stop it!"

"But, Alex—"

"No! Not another word about this. We get in enough trouble without you having any more crazy ideas in your head!"

"HHHEEEEEEYYYYYY!"

I looked up. Mr. Surley, the gym teacher, was standing at the doors. Everybody was heading into the school, and Sam and I were alone in the middle of the schoolyard. We trotted up to the doors and joined the very end of the line going inside.

"Stop!" Mr. Surley ordered. "You two, up against the wall."

He always made me nervous. He was big and had comic-book muscles and always wore sweats and sneakers. He didn't understand me and Sam, and I got the feeling he didn't like things he didn't understand. We stood against the wall and watched the last people disappear into the school while Mr. Surley walked over.

"Office. You need late slips," he said.

"But . . ." I started to protest, but stopped. What was the point?

He held the door open for us and we headed down the hall toward the office. I couldn't be sure, but I thought I heard him chuckling to himself as he walked away in the opposite direction.

Chapter Three

We walked down the hall. Sam hummed to himself—he was oblivious—but I had a lump growing in the pit of my stomach. He'd had a lot more practice going to the office than I did. Besides, Mrs. Watson liked him, and nobody else I knew could say that!

Mrs. Watson was the biggest woman I'd ever seen. She was taller than anybody else in the school, including the male teachers and the janitor. She had big, broad shoulders, large hands and feet and was solidly packed. Not fat, just big. Really big. Mrs. Watson was the mother of the Watson boys. They were all grown up now, but they were still legends in Farmingdale—I guess the way every small town has legends. My father told "Watson boys" stories from when he was little. In those days my school had a Watson boy in every grade from one to seven, but that was way before my time. Everybody said that they had a knack for causing trouble. They were big, there were a lot of them, and they were always daring each other to do crazy things. They also stuck together. My father said if you crossed one of them, you had to deal with all of them.

Mrs. Watson was the only person who could deal with them. There was a rumor she had a tattoo in a place where nobody could see it that read "R.E.S.P.E.C.T." That was something Mrs. Watson got from everybody. Those letters also stood for the first initial of each of her sons' names: Ryan, Edward, Stuart, Peter, Eric, Christopher and Thomas.

It was considered a minor miracle that they eventually turned out so well. They all graduated from high school and went on to college, five of them on football scholarships. They all lived in New York City now, and three of them were policemen. The youngest Watson was a hero to the kids in town because he played professional football for the New York Giants. He was a defensive line guy or defenseman or something like that. I never understood football very well.

We entered the office. Mrs. Watson was bent over, filing something in a drawer, and her enormous backside was aimed at us. Sam cleared his throat.

"Yeah, what do you want?" Mrs. Watson growled as

she turned around. Her face suddenly softened and she rushed around the counter and gave Sam a big hug. "Sammy, what are you doing here? You're not in trouble again, are you?" I tried to hide behind Sam, but that was like hiding a banana behind an apple, since I was a good couple of inches taller than he was, and skinnier.

"Just a little. We were late coming in from recess," Sam answered.

"I see," she said coldly, fixing me with an icy stare.

I suspected that Mrs. Watson didn't like me because she figured every time Sam and I got into trouble it was my fault. She scribbled her signature on two small slips of paper and handed one to each of us.

"Take these back to class, and I don't want to see either of you in here again for a while. Understand?"

I nodded solemnly and Sam smiled broadly. We turned to walk out of the office.

"And Sammy, you be sure to say hello to those darling parents of yours, okay?"

"Sure thing, Mrs. Watson."

Our footsteps echoed off the walls as we walked down the empty hall.

"She really does like your parents, doesn't she," I noted.

"Who?"

"Mrs. Watson, of course!"

"Oh, yeah. For sure. She's been friends with my family since before I was born."

"But I've never seen her at your house before," I commented. I spent so much time at Sam's house that I would have known if she ever visited.

"No. They're not friends like that. My father explained it to me once, but I don't really remember. Something about a loan his bank made to her and her husband."

"I guess that's why she's always so nice to you."

"She's nice to everybody," Sam replied innocently.

"Yeah, right."

The rest of the morning was uneventful. I was sort of looking forward to eating lunch with Twilight, but I was more than a little uneasy about what we'd be talking about. I was also nervous about eating in front of her; my stomach always made lots of gurgling sounds when I ate.

Sam and I walked into the lunchroom. We took a seat at our usual table in the corner with our backs to the wall. It was important to sit with your back to the wall. That's how they killed Wyatt Earp—shot him in the back because he didn't sit in his usual place with his back against the wall. Not that I thought anybody was going to shoot me or anything. You just had to be careful.

Twilight walked into the room with the same girls from our class she'd been talking to at recess. She broke off the conversation with them and came strolling in our direction. Then she took a chair from the far side of our table, dragged it over to our side and pushed it in between us, forcing me to move my chair slightly over to one side.

"The girls wanted me to eat with them but I made an excuse. I told them I wanted to get to know you two better," Twilight said. I couldn't tell if she was serious or making fun of us. Sam and I weren't wildly popular with "the girls."

I looked over at the girls from our class, who'd sat down at a table in the middle of the room. They were all staring at us and giggling. They glanced away when they saw me looking at them. I sort of liked a couple of them but I always had trouble talking to girls. Girls were different from boys. I never knew what to say.

"So tell me, boys, what did you do that got Mr. Roberts so ticked off?"

I put down my milk. Slowly and deliberately I finished chewing on the bite of sandwich in my mouth. "Look, Twilight, you have to know we weren't trying to do anything wrong."

"Sure, sure, that's what I always tell *my* mother."

"No, really! Sam and I have done some things, you know, not bad things or anything."

"Not bad? Is that why Mr. Roberts is so mad at you two?" Twilight teased.

"He's not really mad at us. He likes us," Sam responded.

"I think you're wrong, Sammy. From what I heard, he isn't too crazy about either of you."

"I don't think he could be *that* angry. It was really a neat idea," Sam objected.

"We've been over all of this before, Sam. It was a stupid idea," I snapped.

"Don't argue about it. Just tell me. I'll decide if it was neat or stupid," Twilight interrupted.

"Fine, fine," I agreed. "Well, you know how strict Mrs. Ready is."

"Strict! That doesn't even come close. What's with that list of rules on the board? Does she think this is military school or something?" Twilight said.

"One of those rules is you're not supposed to talk in class," I went on.

"Stupid rule!"

"Well, Sam thought he'd figured out a way for us to talk to each other without her hearing us," I continued.

"But you sit in the back corner and Sam's on the opposite side at the front."

"Yeah, Mrs. Ready split us up because she said she wanted as much real estate between us as the classroom would allow," I explained. "So Sam had us wear these little microphones and earphones—"

"Like secret service agents wear when they're guarding

the president. That's where I got the idea," Sam explained.

"I've seen that on TV. They have, like, tiny microphones on their lapels and a little earphone in their ears. But where did you get them from?" Twilight asked.

"Radio Shack," Sam answered.

"Radio Shack sells things like that?"

"Well, not exactly. He got all the pieces he needed to build them from Radio Shack."

"You can get everything you need to build anything at Radio Shack. Anything!" Sam said. Sam loved Radio Shack the way other kids loved the candy store.

"Wow, that sounds cool!"

"It was cool . . . and neat," Sam added with a smile.

"And stupid. We got caught because it was stupid."

"How did she catch you? Did she hear you talking into the microphones?" Twilight asked.

"Not exactly . . . it had to do with the amplifier or the receiver or whatever you call it," I answered.

"In order to give our units the power to transmit," Sam broke in, "I had to build a special power boost to both pick up signals and transmit them to our earphones."

"And didn't that work?"

"It worked too well," I said, shaking my head.

"How can something work too well?" Twilight asked.

"Because it didn't just pick up our signals, it picked up other signals, too."

"What other signals?"

"Police calls . . . fire department business . . ."

"Wal-Mart announcements," Sam added.

Twilight started chuckling to herself. "So you got all those through your earphones. That's funny."

"But it wasn't just us that heard them," I said. "The amplifier was so powerful it sent all that air traffic into the P.A. system. The whole school heard everything, everything! It was wild!"

"You mean?"

"The whole school heard how there was a special on women's underwear in aisle 5, a code 2–11 in progress at the bakery, and it went on until first recess."

"But why didn't you just turn it off?"

"At first we didn't know it was us causing it, because we hadn't even turned on our microphones when the problems started," Sam answered.

"And that was a good thing, or else everybody in the whole school would have heard us talking," I added.

"When I realized what was going on I wanted to go to my backpack, where the amplifier was, and turn it off, but Mrs. Ready doesn't allow people to leave their seats, so I couldn't."

"How did you get caught?"

"That part was pretty easy," I said, jumping in. "When something like that happens they just come straight to Sam and ask him to explain himself."

"It doesn't seem fair they'd just blame you without any evidence," Twilight objected.

"I guess they didn't need any evidence. They knew that Sam was the only one capable of pulling it off."

"Yeah," Sam noted, "I'm the only genius around here."

"You?" Twilight asked in disbelief. "You're a genius?"

Sam nodded his head in agreement.

"He's not kidding, Twilight. He is an honest-to-goodness genius. They've given him all the tests."

"That's me, a dangerous genius," Sam said with a laugh.

Every time Sam said the word "dangerous" I got a bad feeling. Sam was hard enough to control without his thinking he was dangerous.

Sam stood up and waved. "Hi, Mr. Roberts!" he yelled.

I turned around to see Mr. Roberts standing at the doors. He gave an anxious little wave in reply to Sam and then turned and left the lunchroom.

"See, I told you he likes us," Sam said happily.

"A genius?" Twilight said to me, gesturing to Sam.

"Well . . . not in everything, but who is?"

Twilight nodded approvingly. "So, what else have you boys been up to?"

"We told you our story. Let's hear yours," I replied.

"Okay. What would you like to hear about first? How

about the time I super-glued all the things down on the teacher's desk, or when I replaced the toilet paper in the dispensers with special stuff loaded with itching powder, or when I had the school's telephones and water supply cut off, or when I put rotten meat in the ventilating system, or taped the firecrackers inside the oven in the staff room, or listed the principal's home phone number in the Personals section of *The Village Voice*, or—"

"Enough!" I interrupted. "How about if we just eat lunch and we can talk later." *Much, much later*, I thought. My lunch was just sitting in the pit of my stomach in one big block and it sounded like a whole percussion band was beating out a tune. Thank goodness I always brought along some antacid in my backpack.

Chapter Four

I'd raised my hand to ring the bell when Twilight opened her front door and bounded across the porch and down the steps.

"Come on, guys, we'd better get moving! We don't want to miss anything," she called over her shoulder.

Dressed in jeans hacked off below the knee, an electric-pink T-shirt and a black jean jacket with the sleeves cut out, she dashed down the front path. Sam and I bumped into each other as we turned to follow her.

"Where are we going? What's happening?" I asked nervously.

"It's Saturday, a day for excitement, and there's so much I want to do!"

"There is?" Sam questioned.

"Yes! The only hard part is I don't know where to start. There are just so many choices!"

"So many choices . . ." Sam echoed vacantly.

Twilight kept up her pace and we struggled to keep up with her, one on each side. I was working up a sweat. She was moving so fast I didn't have a chance to take off the extra wool sweater I'd put on that morning to avoid catching a chill.

"I just don't know. Should we go down to McKee's store and play the video game, or head for the highway and wave at the passing trucks to see if we can get them to honk their horns? Or, if you two can handle all the excitement, maybe we should stand right by the traffic light and watch it change from green to yellow to red to green. Or we could stare at the poster at the movie theater. Or, if we're early enough, maybe we can watch them unroll the sidewalks!" It was only at the end that the sarcasm took over her voice.

"Very funny," I answered.

Twilight sat down on the bench outside the barbershop. "Oh wow! I was so afraid all the good seats would be taken—after all, this is the very *heart* of downtown!"

I would have argued about that, but she was right. This was the intersection of the two main streets.

"Sitting here we can see traffic in all directions, as well as watching people getting their hair cut. I know it's one of the highlights!"

"There are other things to do," I protested.

"Like what?"

Unfortunately I didn't have an answer available.

"Could we start at McKee's?" Sam asked. "I really like the new video game he just got in. Have either of you played it yet?"

Twilight just shook her head, amazed that Sam hadn't figured out this was just another one of her tirades against Farmingdale. They'd been coming more and more regularly for the past two weeks. It was as though it had just sunk in for Twilight that she wasn't just visiting, she was actually living here. I guess I really couldn't blame her. She'd lived around the world in places like London, Paris, New York and L.A. Compared with them, Farmingdale, with its ten thousand people, must have seemed awfully small and dull.

"It's not so bad here." I felt somebody had to defend our town.

"Give me a break, Alex. I've heard your whole speech about what a wonderful little town this is. How *friendly and clean and safe*," she said, mocking my voice.

"Well, it is safe. A lot safer than the city."

"Are you kidding? Safer, hah! I nearly died here yesterday," she replied.

"You did? How?" Sam asked.

"I nearly died of boredom."

I hadn't known Twilight long, but long enough to

know there was no point in arguing with her. I had to change the direction of the conversation.

"So, what exciting thing would you be doing if you were in the city right now?" I asked.

"Nothing . . . right now."

"So what's the difference between nothing there and nothing here?" I asked.

"Because nothing there would have led to *something*. Something for all of us."

She had my attention now. I had a feeling something interesting was coming.

Slowly and very deliberately she rose to her feet and pulled from her pocket a small envelope. "Later, we'd be using these," she said.

She handed me the envelope and I pulled out four tickets. Front-row floor seats to a rock concert—the biggest concert of the season, six very hot bands—for the following weekend at Madison Square Garden.

"Wow!" I said before I could stop myself. "Where did you get these? That concert is sold out. It's been sold out for weeks."

"They're a present from my father. He gets free tickets all the time, because he's a celebrity. He got them so that he could take me and my two new friends to the concert."

"New friends . . . like us?" I asked.

"Do you see anybody else crowding the streets of

downtown Farmingdale?" Twilight replied. For one reason or another, Twilight had been spending most of her time hanging out with us. I guess it was partly that the other girls were having trouble figuring her out—her big-city attitude and weird clothes and hair. She didn't seem to fit into any of their cliques.

"That's . . . that's great!" I turned to Sam. "We're going to New York to—"

"You *were* going," Twilight said, cutting me off.

My head snapped around. "You're not taking us?"

"I'm not going. None of us are going."

"But . . . but . . ." I held up the tickets.

"My father can't go. He has to go out of town for a promotional tour. He visits shopping malls and signs autographs for ladies who live for the soap operas. And because he's gone, we can't go," Twilight explained. "I almost didn't tell you guys."

"I wish you hadn't," I admitted.

"So I guess I shouldn't tell you the rest of what was going to happen."

"There's more?" I wanted to hear, but I didn't want to know.

"My mom was going to be calling your parents. My father asked if we could stay for the weekend. He was going to send a car to get us and—"

"Like a limousine?" I asked.

"Just a small one. The studio has them. They don't even

have a bar or anything. He was going to send a car up to get us after school on Friday. We'd stay in his apartment Friday night, and then he'd take us around New York all day Saturday before the concert. And since the concert would be late, we'd sleep over again Saturday night and come back on Sunday."

"In the limousine again?" Sam asked.

She nodded.

"And now . . . now none of this is going to happen."

"None," Twilight said.

We sat in silence. I watched the traffic light change from red to green. A mother, leading her little boy by the hand, opened the door of the barbershop and the bell rang to announce their arrival.

"I probably shouldn't have told you guys anything about this," Twilight said. "I didn't want you to be upset, or think that my father was a jerk for canceling."

"We don't think he's a jerk," I said. "Things come up sometimes, I guess."

She snorted. "I wish it was just sometimes. This is twice this month. Boy, is my mom going to be angry."

"Going to be?" I asked.

"Yeah. She doesn't know yet. He called last night and told me himself. My parents don't talk at all. If one has a message to give to the other they pass it on through me."

"That must be hard, being caught in the middle," I said.

"It's better than being in the middle of a fight. Besides, it has its up side." She gave a little smile. "I only pass on the messages I want to pass on." Twilight took the tickets back from me. "Too bad, though. You can't get any better seats in the whole of the Garden," I observed.

"The Garden!" Apparently those were the magic words with the power to bring Sam back to the land of the living. "Madison Square Garden? Let me see those tickets!" He grabbed them out of her hand and examined them closely.

Sam was going to be an architect when he grew up. He wanted to design buildings. Other kids had posters of their favorite sports stars on their bedroom walls. Sam had pictures of buildings he liked. And Madison Square Garden was one of his favorites. He even had a full copy of the blueprints of the building. I'd been with Sam and his father to a couple of Rangers games, but it wasn't about hockey for Sam. He just waited for the intermissions so we could walk around the building and examine the structure.

"We really *should* go," Sam said.

"We can't go. Weren't you listening to anything we said?" Twilight asked.

"No, not really," Sam replied.

Big surprise.

We sat on the bench in silence. There was a chill in the air; we were definitely into fall weather. I watched the traffic light turn from red to green to yellow to red and back to green. If we sat there long enough, I figured we'd watch the leaves turn from green to yellow and red too. I rummaged in one of my pockets. I could feel a couple of quarters. Maybe we could go to McKee's and play the video game, my treat.

Sam broke the silence. "I don't know how, exactly, but I think we should use these tickets."

Twilight looked at Sam. She probably thought this was just idle talk. She didn't know him the way I did.

"Just let me think for a little while . . . just let me think," Sam said. He stood up and pulled out his idea book, which he always carried, folded, in his back pocket. He opened it up and sat back down.

I knew the trouble I'd seen in the distance was almost on top of us. I could smell the storm in the air, almost see the clouds start to cluster in the sky.

Sam found an empty page and pulled a pen out of the front pocket of his pants. Instantly he started making notes.

"What is he doing?" Twilight asked.

"He's trying to figure out a way to get to the concert," I explained without even needing to ask.

"And he already has an idea?" Twilight had never really seen Sam in action before. It was pretty intense.

I shook my head. "Not yet. He's probably just writing down the problem and the independent variables associated with—"

"The what?"

"Independent variables. The things involved with the problem," I said. "He's treating this like it's a big science problem or a math equation and he's trying to figure out the answer."

"He's wasting his time," she said.

That was what I was hoping. I kept telling Sam that life wasn't a mathematics question and that some things didn't have answers.

"You know," I said, "even if your father hadn't gone out of town, we still probably wouldn't have been able to go to the concert."

"Why not?"

"My mother hates rock concerts. She says nothing but bad stuff can happen at places like that. I probably won't be able to go to one until I'm a teenager—a really *old* teenager."

"That's stupid."

"That's parents. Not just mine. Sam's parents feel the same way."

"Is everybody in this town stupid or is it just my—?"

"I have an idea," Sam announced.

"What?" I exclaimed. This was fast, even for him.

"I think I have it figured out."

"No, hold on. I don't like it!" I told him.

"What do you mean you don't like it?" Sam protested. "You haven't even *heard* it."

"I don't need to hear it to know I don't like it. Every time you get that look in your eye we end up in big trouble."

"But I'm confident—" Sam began.

"The more *confident* you are, the bigger the trouble," I interrupted again.

"Be fair, Alex," Sam pleaded.

"Yeah, Alex, be fair," Twilight echoed.

"Fair! Be fair!" I practically yelled. "Was it fair when he talked me into dyeing my dog red last Valentine's Day?" I could feel the veins on my neck bulge and my eyes bug out.

"You dyed your dog?" Twilight sounded amazed.

I nodded my head and shrugged.

"He sure looked pretty," Sam said. "Besides, I was right."

"What do you mean you were right?" I demanded.

"I told you it would impress the girls in our class, and it did," Sam explained.

"Who were you trying to impress?" Twilight asked coyly.

"Nobody," I lied. "But the person it really impressed was my mother when we couldn't wash out the dye."

"Wait," Twilight interrupted, "I've seen your dog. His fur is scruffy, but he definitely isn't red. The dye *must* have come out."

"We . . . um . . . shaved the dog," Sam answered, so quietly he could hardly be heard.

"What did you say?"

"We shaved him," I repeated. "Right down to the skin. Most pathetic sight I ever saw in my whole life. Try to picture him bald."

"How long are you going to hold that against me?" Sam asked. "Everybody's entitled to one little mistake."

"One mistake!" I yelled, as I jumped up from the bench. "One mistake! Let's not forget last Christmas when we roasted those chestnuts in my microwave and blew the door off. Or the time we dug up my back lawn because your metal detector 'beeped' that gold was buried there. Or the time we took apart my father's gas lawn mower because it didn't work, when all that was wrong was it was out of gas. Or the time—"

"Okay, okay," Sam interrupted. "I admit, not all of my plans have been perfect. But this one is. Just let me explain."

"NO!" I shouted. "I don't, I repeat, *don't*, want to hear it."

"Be reasonable. What have you got to lose by listening?" Sam asked.

"He's got a point, Alex," Twilight said. "It can't hurt to just hear him out."

"Twilight, you don't understand. I've known Sam my entire life. He's my best friend, so believe me on this: no matter how stupid or lamebrained his idea is, he'll make it sound wonderful. If we let him talk, in just a few minutes we'll be slapping him on the back and telling him it's the greatest idea in the world."

Twilight shot me a look of total disgust. "Give me a break, Alex. I'm not some small-town *hick*," she said, taking a shot at both me and Farmingdale. "I've lived in cities my whole life. I know a thing or two. I've had *experiences*. Nobody, and I mean nobody, could talk me into doing something *stupid* or *lamebrained*."

"Yeah, Alex, give her credit," Sam echoed, as he tried to hide the smile creeping onto his face.

I knew I was trapped.

"Okay," Sam began, "first we need to use my computer . . ."

Five minutes later both Twilight and I slapped Sam on the back and told him his plan was the greatest idea in the world.

Chapter Five

It took us a few days to pull the plan together, but by Tuesday we were ready to face one of our biggest hurdles: Sam's parents. They would have to be handled delicately. And the time was now, because Sam's dad had just got home from the bank where he worked.

The front door opened and footsteps echoed on the hall floor before he stuck his head into the living room.

"Hi, Sam, Alex. How are things?" he asked.

"It was an interesting day," Sam answered.

"Yes, sir," I agreed.

Mr. Sterling put down his briefcase. A worried look crept onto his face. "Okay, boys, just how interesting was it, and what kind of trouble did you two get into?"

"They didn't get into any trouble at all," Mrs. Sterling said as she came up the stairs from the basement, carrying the laundry. "You really are becoming a little paranoid, dear."

"With good reason," he answered. He loosened his tie. "What was so *interesting*?"

"We were invited to go away for the weekend."

"Go where, with who?" Mr. Sterling asked. He didn't sound thrilled.

"To New York with Twilight." I could see Sam bracing himself for the next bit. "To go to a rock concert."

"New York? And who exactly is this Twilight girl?"

"She's the new girl," Sam said.

"You've met her," Mrs. Sterling said. "Remember?"

He got a confused look on his face—the same look I'd seen on Sam's hundreds of times. "Sure . . . okay . . . I remember," he said, although I was sure he didn't.

"Her mother called today," Mrs. Sterling said. "I've talked to her before at the grocery store. She seems like a very nice lady."

"And she's taking you kids into the city for the weekend?" Mr. Sterling asked.

"Not her. We'd be going with Twilight's father."

"And the mother wouldn't be going?"

"They're separated, dear," Mrs. Sterling explained.

Mr. Sterling shook his head sadly.

"That's why they moved out here," Sam told him.

"It's been hard for Twilight. That's why Alex and I have tried to be good friends to her. I think it helps her a lot."

"I just don't know about this concert," Mr. Sterling said. "What do you think?" he asked his wife.

"I think it would be all right. Mrs. Stevens assures me that her husband will be with them at all times. Apparently he's somewhat overprotective of his daughter."

"There's no such thing as *over*protective," Mr. Sterling said.

"And she says that the concert tickets will probably be in a special section, some sort of VIP area. Twilight's father is an actor, after all." It was lucky for us that Sam's mother liked to tape *These Days Are Forever* and watch it at night—her "guilty pleasure," she called it.

"Oh, that's right, he's some sort of TV soap star, isn't he?"

"Just because he's an actor doesn't mean he isn't a good person and a good parent," Mrs. Sterling pointed out.

Sam must have sensed that the plan was going off the rails, so he jumped in. "But, Dad, if you don't want me to go, that's okay," Sam said. "Aside from the concert, it'll probably be pretty boring anyway."

"It will?" Mr. Sterling asked.

"Yeah. Twilight's father is really into art and stuff. Twilight said the whole weekend might be nothing more than him dragging us from one museum and art gallery to another."

"That doesn't sound boring to me," Mrs. Sterling said.

"Me either," her husband agreed.

"I always think it's a shame that we're only a two-hour drive from New York but we don't take full advantage of its wonderful, world-class culture," Mrs. Sterling added.

"So what did your parents have to say about all of this?" Mr. Sterling asked me.

"They didn't have any objections," I said. That was because they knew nothing about it, so they'd had no chance to object.

"Your parents are pretty reasonable people," Mr. Sterling said.

"It would mean a lot," Sam added. "Not just to us, but to Twilight. I know it's been pretty hard for her to fit in . . . what with the separation and all."

"Well . . ." Mr. Sterling looked at his wife. She nodded.

"So can I go?" Sam asked.

"Of course you can, Sam." Mr. Sterling said, beaming.

"And we're very proud of you," chimed in Mrs. Sterling. "It's just wonderful the way you and Alex have taken that little girl under your wing and helped her to fit in. We're proud of *both* of you."

I started nodding my head hard in agreement. I must have looked like one of those little plastic dogs sitting in the back of a car window.

"Maybe we should start to throw a few things into a suitcase. Friday is only three days away," noted Mrs. Sterling.

"Could I use a backpack instead of a suitcase, Mom?" Sam asked.

"A backpack?"

"Yeah, Mrs. Sterling, we thought it would be more cool. We were talking about it and Twilight said that's what the kids in the city use—what she's going to use—and we wouldn't want her to feel bad if we had something different."

"Sounds okay with me. If you two think it's more *cool*, then so be it," Mrs. Sterling said.

"I was thinking I could just use my school backpack," Sam said.

"Is that big enough?"

"Sure. We're not going away for that long."

"Sounds like a plan," Mr. Sterling said. "I'll just give your parents a call, Alex, and we can discuss some of the—"

"No!" I practically screamed. "I mean, no . . . there's no point in calling them because they're not home right now. I'll get them to call you tonight, though."

My parents were probably home already. I just didn't want him to talk to them yet—at least not until I'd talked to them and explained that Sam's parents were going along with it.

"But if you do have any questions about anything you could talk to Twilight's mother. She'd be really happy to talk to you about the whole thing."

There was no danger there. As far as she was concerned it was all true. It wouldn't be the first time that Twilight's dad had sent a limo to bring her to the city for the weekend. And Twilight had neglected to tell her about the call from her father canceling all the plans. Since her parents hadn't talked for over six months and, according to her mother, weren't planning on *ever* talking again, we figured we'd be safe.

"Oh, we're definitely going to talk to her as well," Mr. Sterling said.

"And, of course, Twilight's father," Mrs. Sterling said.

"That might be more difficult," Sam said. Both his parents gave him a questioning look. "Twilight will give you the number, but he's supposed to be famous for not returning calls. He gets hundreds and hundreds of them from his fans. He can't take the time to talk to all of them. But Twilight says he's a great guy."

"Yeah, Twilight says he's great," I said.

"I'm sure he is," Mr. Sterling replied—although his tone was saying the opposite.

"Now, if you boys will excuse me, I'm going to get myself a cold drink," Mr. Sterling said. He went into the kitchen.

"And we'd better get upstairs and start packing," Sam said to his mother. "Alex can help me. I wouldn't want to leave it to the last minute."

"That's good thinking, planning in advance," Mrs. Sterling remarked.

Mr. Sterling came back into the room, holding a can of Coke. "Say, Alex, what time will your parents be home?"

"Probably around six."

"It's after six right now. I should call your father and—"

"Did I say six? I meant seven. Maybe even seven-thirty. My father is working on a big ad account, and he's been putting in a lot of long hours."

"Your father always works long hours. He's one of the hardest-working people I know," Mr. Sterling said.

"That's my dad."

"We'd better get packing, Alex," Sam said.

"Yeah, we should."

We stumbled up the stairs and into Sam's room. I caught sight of myself in the mirror above his dresser. My face was white and I could see a few beads of sweat on my forehead.

"That was close," I said quietly.

"Close only counts in horseshoes and hand grenades," Sam countered.

"Very funny."

"We knew that if your parents agreed, then my parents would agree, and if my parents agreed, then your parents would agree. We just had to give one of them a nudge first."

"That wasn't a nudge. That was a lie. A lie that almost got us caught," I argued.

"It's only going to be a lie until you talk to your parents. Once they know my parents have agreed, they'll say yes as well and—"

The phone rang, cutting Sam off. It was his phone—his private line that rang only in his room. Sam's parents had agreed to it when he started tying up the phone for hours with his Internet downloads. Sam picked up the phone.

"Hello . . . yes . . ." he said.

"Is it Twilight?" I asked.

He nodded. "Hang on," he said into the phone. He reached down and pushed a button on the base of the phone and put the receiver down.

"Hi again, Twilight. You're on the speakerphone now," Sam said. "Say hello to Alex."

"Hi, Alex. How did it go?"

"Pretty good," I answered. "How about with you, Twilight?"

"All according to plan. She still doesn't know anything. As far as she's concerned, my father will send a car to pick us up from school on Friday and drive us into New York. We'll go to the concert, do some other stuff, and then we'll be brought home safe and sound on Sunday morning."

"That reminds me," I said. "Just how exactly are we really getting to and from New York?"

"I've got that worked out," Twilight said.

"So just *what* do you have worked out?" I asked.

"If I told you it would ruin the surprise! Have faith, Alex. Sammy isn't the only genius around here."

"And your mother still has no idea?" I asked. I was worried about what would happen when Sam's parents—or *my* parents—called to speak to her.

"Why should she? It's business as usual. Besides, I'm pretty good at keeping a secret . . . or telling a lie."

"I guess part of that should be reassuring," I said.

"All of it. I never tell lies to my friends. Just my family. So, you had no problem at your end?"

"Hey, no problem here," Sam answered.

I was thinking it was more like "no pulse" rather than "no problem," but I wasn't going to get into it.

"And you, Alex?"

"I still have to talk to my parents, but now that Sam's parents have signed off, it should be all systems go."

"Then all we have to do is pack and wait," Twilight said.

"Yeah . . . pack . . . wait . . . and worry," I agreed.

Chapter Six

The alarm clock rang to signal the start of the day. I reached over and turned it off. It hadn't woken me because I'd been up for the past two hours, lying in the dark, staring at the clock, thinking about what was going to happen. I thought about all the things that *could* go wrong. Things I was sure *would* go wrong.

Meanwhile, I knew neither Sam nor Twilight had lost any sleep. Sam would have slept the sleep of the totally innocent and trusting. Twilight would have a better idea about the potential for disaster, but she probably wouldn't care if the whole thing exploded in our faces. For her, it was all just an adventure, whether it worked or not.

Even worse, I'd been starting to suspect that she *liked* it when things went wrong. The stories she liked telling the most were the ones where she crash-landed. That made me even more nervous.

I picked up my bag. We had to take enough clothes and things to satisfy our parents that we were going away for the weekend, but not enough to make anybody at school suspicious. That was why the backpacks were so important, because we couldn't very well go to school carrying suitcases without somebody being tipped off. I unbuckled the backpack and did a final check. I had two changes of clothes, including socks and underwear, my favorite T-shirt, an extra pair of shoes, toothpaste, toothbrush, dental floss, the puffer for my asthma, special ointment for my nose in case it started to bleed, some antacid, children's aspirin and a thermometer. I didn't like to go anywhere without a thermometer. I worried a lot about getting sick. Even my own mother said I was getting to be an old woman, worrying about my health, and she made me stop reading medical books. Well, she could stop me from reading, but she couldn't stop me from worrying.

Next I took my wallet off the dresser. I opened it up and checked the money one more time. Between the money my parents had given me for the trip and my savings, I had almost sixty bucks. I knew Sam would take about the same amount, and Twilight was going to take even more than that.

I got up and went to my bathroom. The humidifier sat on the counter, puffing out a steamy cloud of mist. I took a deep breath. My sinuses were clear and fine this morning. I splashed water on my face. I was in no rush to get downstairs. I wanted to time it so my parents would be just going out the door as I got to the kitchen.

"ALEX! Get moving, sleepyhead!" my mother yelled up the stairs. "We're just getting ready to leave!"

Selling my parents on the weekend away had turned out to be pretty easy. Of course, they'd talked to Sam's "no such thing as *over*protective" dad, and they'd phoned Twilight's mom for the details. But after that, they were fairly easygoing about it. It was almost scary how simple this was turning out to be.

I grabbed my backpack and went downstairs. My mother was piling the breakfast dishes in the sink and my father was standing by the counter, downing the last bit of his orange juice. He put his glass in the sink as well.

"Morning, Alex. All excited about your big weekend?" my father asked.

"Very," I answered.

"Nervous?"

"A little," I admitted.

"There's nothing to be nervous about, so don't worry . . . either of you," my father offered reassuringly as he came over and put a hand on my mother's shoulder.

Boy, was he wrong. There was plenty to be nervous about. Plenty!

"Okay?" he asked.

"Yes." I was trying my best to sound convincing.

"We'd better get going. Be sure to lock up when you leave, okay?" my father reminded me.

I nodded in agreement. My mother came over and gave me a big hug.

"I know you'll be okay, Alex. It's just that I'm a bit worried about you going away by yourself for the weekend. But I know you're not my little boy any more. You're a young man. A *responsible* young man," she said.

I was hit by a pang of guilt.

"We know we can count on you, Alex," my father said, offering me an even bigger dose of guilt. He joined in and wrapped his arms around both me and my mother.

We all said our goodbyes and they hurried out the door. I went to the window and watched as they climbed into the car. They both worked in an office just outside of New York. I was going to follow the same route as they did today, but it wasn't going to be by car. We were taking a bus—Twilight had checked the schedule and bought the tickets—that would take us from Farmingdale right into the heart of New York City.

My father backed the car out of the driveway, and as it started forward my mother waved out the window. I watched as the car drove away and then turned the corner and was gone. It was funny, but I felt a strange combination of relief and anxiety. I'd been harboring this fantasy that they knew all about our plan and at the last minute they'd spring it on me. I pictured my father saying something like *Well, young man, did you really think you could get away with it? We'll see you right after school, and you're grounded for the entire weekend!* I didn't want to spend the weekend in my room, but at least it would be safe in there. Much safer than where we were going.

I'd been to the city lots of times before—I wasn't a total hick—but never without an adult. The city was a very big, loud, grungy, scary place—nice to visit, but I was always glad to get home again.

I rushed back into the kitchen and grabbed a piece of cold toast and my backpack. I hated being alone in the house and I wanted to get out as quickly as possible. Stuffing the toast into my mouth, I fled through the door. I sprinted down the path and then put on the brakes, walked back and checked the door. It was locked, just as it was every morning when I went back to check.

I hurried off and then stopped again when I realized my laces needed to be tied. I bent down. Looking back, I saw my house. It was a nice house, a comfortable house, a safe house. I had this awful, eerie moment, wondering if I'd ever see it again.

"Don't be so stupid!" I said out loud.

Sam's house was just around the corner. I cut across his lawn and up onto his porch. I hesitated before I knocked at the door. Sam's mother had said I should treat their home like my home, and there was no need for me to knock on my own door. But my mother had told me it was polite to knock. To please both of them, I always knocked on the door first and then walked in. I went straight to the kitchen, where Sam and his parents were seated around the table, eating breakfast. I took a seat at the breakfast table as well. There was a cereal bowl, side plate, glass and utensils, all ready for me.

Mr. and Mrs. Sterling were having an involved conversation, and other than a nod from both, they ignored me and continued their discussion. As best as I could make out, they were arguing about the government and inflation.

I dipped a spoon into the bowl, which was filled with oat bran cereal. A couple of dried prunes peeked through the flakes. Mrs. Sterling was very big into bran cereals and prunes. She believed they were the keys to keeping the whole family regular. As I'd heard her say so often, *Happy bowels make for happy boys*. Sam hated bran cereals and only wanted to eat the kinds with sugar in them. I ate the stuff up, though—I was on his mother's side if it meant being healthy.

"Good gracious!" Mrs. Sterling said with a start.

"Look at the time! We have to get going right now or we'll be late!"

Mr. Sterling glanced at his watch as he and his wife jumped up from the table.

"Sam, Alex, I'm sorry we got sidetracked this morning. We were so involved in our discussion we just ignored the two of you," Mr. Sterling apologized.

"Yes, we did want to talk about your weekend away, but now we don't have time," Mrs. Sterling added.

"That's okay, Mom, Dad, there'll be plenty of time to talk about it after we get back," Sam told them.

"And Twilight's father will pick you up at the end of the school day, right?" Mrs. Sterling asked.

"Not him. His driver," Sam said. "End of the day, right in front of the office."

Soon we were all on our way. Mr. Sterling drove off in one direction, Mrs. Sterling in the other. Weighed down by our backpacks, we set off for school.

"Did you lock the door?" I asked as we started down the street.

"I don't know," Sam answered.

"You don't know? Maybe we'd better go back and check!"

"Naah. Don't worry about it."

"But what if somebody breaks into your house?" I couldn't believe he wasn't even a little concerned.

"Won't happen," Sam replied calmly.

"How can you be so sure?"

"For one thing, since I probably left the door open they won't have to break in. And besides, there's no crime in Farmingdale, so don't worry."

I knew there was no point in trying to argue with him.

"It was lucky your parents were too busy talking to ask us any more questions."

"No luck involved," Sam replied with a smile. "When we sat down for breakfast I asked my father if he thought the president was doing a good job. They were fighting about it before I could put the first spoonful of cereal in my mouth."

Up ahead I saw Twilight standing with her backpack, waiting for us. She was tapping her foot impatiently. She checked her watch and then fixed us with a disdainful look. Considering how she was always keeping us waiting, I didn't know what right she had to be upset.

"I thought you two had chickened out and I'd have to go solo," she offered as a greeting.

"Not us," I replied. "We were just hoping *you* hadn't backed out," I lied. I'd hoped, and prayed, that somehow, for some reason, she had changed her mind and I could escape with my pride intact. One more escape route gone.

"Did your mom have any last-minute suspicions?" I asked, trying to restart the conversation in a friendlier direction.

"No, none. She was too busy fighting with me. First thing this morning I told her I'd changed my mind and I wasn't going to go to my father's," Twilight said casually.

"You told her what?" I responded with a start.

"Told her I wasn't going to go."

"But . . . but . . ." I stammered.

"She got so mad she practically threw me and my bag on the porch. She told me we weren't even going to talk about it any more because I was going whether I liked it or not. I argued a little more, gave in to her in the end and then left."

"Pretty smooth," Sam said.

"Smooth?" I said. "Why didn't you want to go?"

"I *did* want to go, Alex, darling. That's why I told her I didn't," she explained.

"But then why did you . . . ?"

"Reverse psychology," Sam said. "Tell your parents one thing so they'll make you do the opposite. Really smart."

"Really dangerous," I disagreed. "What if she'd agreed with you and said you didn't have to go?"

"Give me a break, Alex," Twilight said. "How often do parents ever agree with anything that we say?"

School was long and slow. Even longer and slower than usual. I found it almost impossible to concentrate on anything. My mind was filled with what was going to be happening, and, more important, all the things that could go wrong. I'd mentioned my worries to Sam. He said I should be more positive. I tried. Now I was *positive* bad things were going to happen. While everybody else worked on creative writing, I wrote down the order in which things would happen:

1. We will leave.
2. It will be a great adventure.
3. We will have an interesting and maybe fun time.
4. We will get caught and get in big trouble, OR, we will get in big trouble and then get caught.

The strange thing was, writing things down made me feel better. I now knew we'd get caught and I didn't have to worry nearly as much any more. I figured there was no sense in worrying because, in the end, we were dead.

On and off through the day I watched Twilight and Sam. At lunch and during recess they were both so excited I was afraid one of them might explode. I struggled hard not to be drawn into the excitement. Somebody had to stay calm.

I looked at the clock on the wall. In just a few more minutes the bell would ring and we'd be off. I was positive I could hear it ticking from across the room. I focused all my energy on that clock. If I could magically stop the second hand from moving, the time wouldn't change, and if the time didn't change, then the bell wouldn't ring, and if the bell didn't ring we wouldn't leave school, and if we didn't leave school we couldn't go away and if we couldn't go away we'd all be safe and . . .

RRRRRRRIIIIIIIIIIIIIINNNNNNNNGGGGGG!

I jumped into the air. Everybody looked at me. Mrs. Ready scowled. The class waited for her to give the signal that we could leave.

"Class dismissed."

Now I was engulfed by the sounds of scraping chairs, shuffling papers and kids talking and kidding around as they escaped out the door for the weekend. I grabbed my backpack and Sam did the same. We both headed for the door. Twilight followed close behind.

We walked to the front of the school and went out through the main entrance. We didn't normally go that way, but we wanted to make sure one of our parents hadn't dropped by to see us off before we could get away. The last thing we needed was for one of them to wait with us for a driver who wasn't coming. We looked all around. Nobody was there except for the usual bustle of kids, cars and parents. We walked off school property, crossed the street and headed for the ravine. Sam and I had figured out the best possible route to follow. The ravine took us around the outskirts of the town, where we were less likely to run into anybody we knew. I glanced back nervously as I got ready to step down into the ravine. Nobody was there to see anything. I hurried to catch up to Sam and Twilight and stumbled on an exposed tree root, almost falling on my face.

Twilight had purchased our bus tickets the day before from Mrs. Jenkins who ran Drapery and Stuff, which doubled as the bus station in town. We knew if either Sam or I went in to buy tickets word would get back to our parents in a few hours. Twilight was still pretty much unknown. That just meant Mrs. Jenkins knew who she was, because in this town you quickly got to know everybody, but didn't know her mother well enough to strike up a conversation.

Coming out of the ravine we found ourselves in position, by the highway. In town the bus only made scheduled stops, but on the highway it would stop for anybody who flagged it down. We backtracked a few feet so the trees would hide us from passing cars. We didn't want to risk being seen standing on the highway. I looked at my watch. We still had twenty minutes before the bus would arrive. I took a seat on a log and Sam sat down beside me.

"So far, so good," I noted.

"We still have one more potential problem. A huge problem," Twilight said dramatically.

"Problem, what problem?"

"Well, when we get on the bus there might be somebody who'll recognize one of you two. You know, a neighbor or a friend or something," she explained.

"Gee, I hadn't thought of that." I wanted to suggest that maybe we should call the whole thing off, but I knew that wouldn't fly.

"Never fear, gentlemen. I *have* thought about it, and I have a way to guarantee nobody will recognize you." With a flourish she pulled two wigs from her bag, one with long blond hair and the other with shorter brown.

"Alex, you put on the blond wig, and Sam, the other one is for you," Twilight announced.

"You've got to be kidding . . ." I mumbled in shock.

"Kidding? No, I'm not kidding, but if you really want, Alex, you can wear the brunette wig. Although, I have to tell you, you really have the complexion to be a blond."

Twilight reached into her bag again and pulled out two fluffy, feminine-looking sweaters, one pink and one blue. She held them up for us to see.

"Aren't they pretty . . . disgusting? I love my nana, but she's always getting me things like this so I can dress more like a lady," Twilight explained. "It would be better if you pulled on the sweater before the wig. I think the pink one goes best with the blond wig, so this one's for you," Twilight announced, as she tried to hand the sweater to me.

I refused to take it. "Twilight, do you think we're crazy? We're not going to dress like girls!" I was sounding pretty seriously defiant until my voice cracked on the last word. I got to my feet.

"No, Alex, I don't think you two are crazy, but I do think you want to get on the bus, and if somebody recognizes either one of you, we're dead in the water. I'm just trying to help," she answered.

Her voice caught on the last few words, like she was about to cry. A few weeks ago that might have worked. Now, knowing her as I did, I knew she could even coax out a few tears for the right occasion, and I wasn't going to be fooled by her acting. I turned to Sam, still seated calmly on the log.

"It's not just me, you know, Twilight. Sam, tell her there's no way you're going to put on that brown wig and sweater."

There was a long pause. Sam had taken the wig and sweater from Twilight and was holding them in his hands, looking at them. "He's right. I'm not putting on either of these."

"See?" I said triumphantly.

"I want to wear the blond wig and the pink sweater," Sam said. "I've always heard that blonds have more fun, and I want to have more fun!"

My mouth dropped open and I stood there, stunned.

Sam handed me the wig and sweater he was holding and took the others from Twilight. She helped him pull on the pink sweater and settle the wig over his straight brown hair. She tucked in the little bits of his hair sticking out from under the front.

"Come on, Alex, get moving! We only have a few minutes until the bus arrives," Twilight prodded.

With a feeling of total disgust I dropped the wig on top of my backpack and pulled the sweater on over my shirt. Twilight, now finished with Sam, came over and started to smooth it down. She picked up the wig and placed it on my head, turned it around and pulled it tighter. Finally she poked in a couple of pieces of my hair that must have been trying to escape.

"I was right," she said, shaking her head in dismay.

"You were right about what?" I asked.

"You would have made a better-looking blond. Now for the final touch."

Twilight reached into her purse.

"A little bit of make-up," she sang.

I felt a shudder go through my entire body. I wanted to argue, to fight, to run away, to scream. Instead I puckered my lips as Twilight applied the lipstick. I'd always figured the first time a girl's lipstick touched my lips it would be slightly more romantic.

"THERE IT IS!" Sam yelled. He was standing by the road, looking back toward town.

"Where, where is it?" Twilight asked excitedly.

Sam ran back over to where we stood. "Top of the hill. It just pulled up to Drapery and Stuff to pick up the passengers and parcels."

Quickly, Twilight applied a little lipstick and rouge to Sam. Putting away the make-up in her purse, she pulled out the tickets and handed one to each of us. We watched the bus slowly pull away from the store and gain speed. When it was about twenty-five yards up the road, we left the shelter of the ravine and ran to the shoulder. The bus was accelerating and gaining momentum as it came down the hill. We waved our arms, holding our tickets aloft.

The bus screamed past, quickly followed by a blast of wind and a wave of gravel and grit, which stung as it hit my face. Almost immediately I heard the sound of the air brakes before it pulled off the road. The gravel crunched under the wheels as it came to a stop, and we sprinted after it. The big front door opened. Twilight jumped on, followed by Sam and then me.

"Sorry, girls," the driver apologized. "I almost missed you. I could have sworn nobody was there."

"That's okay, sir," Twilight answered sweetly. "The important thing is that you did stop. Our parents would have been so worried if we didn't get off this bus at the station in New York in time to make it home for dinner."

We handed our tickets to the driver and made our way

to the back of the bus. Before we'd got to the back, the driver pulled away, and we swayed and rocked our way down the aisle. I dropped my head, eyes staring at the floor. We slumped into seats at the very back.

Twilight smiled. "Well, girls, we're on our way."

Chapter Seven

Sam sat in the corner at the back, right against the window. Twilight sat down beside him and I took the aisle seat so I could stretch out my legs. I had a view right down the middle of the bus all the way through the front windshield. With my sensitive stomach it was important that I could see where I was going. And probably handy that I was right next to the toilet. I fumbled around underneath me.

"What are you doing?" Twilight asked.

"Trying to find the seat belt," I answered, turning around and looking more carefully.

Twilight took me by the arm and pulled me back into my seat. "Alex, this is a bus—there aren't any seat belts."

"No seat belts! That's dangerous! What if we get into a crash?"

"We're in a bus, Alex. A big bus. I think we're safe unless we hit something bigger . . . like an ocean liner or an iceberg," Twilight answered sarcastically.

I settled in my seat. There was no point in arguing.

A look down the aisle confirmed my first impression: the bus was practically empty. That made sense, because we were heading into the city in the afternoon when everybody else was rushing in the other direction.

The bus was a big coach, all orange on the outside with the logo of the Tri-City Coach Lines. I'd watched their buses going through our town ever since I could remember. They roared down the main street, fumes belching out of the exhaust, stopping only long enough at Drapery and Stuff to pick up packages and passengers. A couple of times I'd been right there when they'd pulled in. I was amazed at how big they were and how high above the ground the people were as they looked out the windows.

My attention turned to Sam, who had started to tinker with things. He lowered the serving tray from the chair in front of him. Then he reached over Twilight and released the one in front of her and it clanked down, hitting her on the knees. She cursed under her breath and I pushed it back into place. Sam didn't notice. Next he turned on his individual reading lamp and adjusted the air-conditioning vent. He took a fingernail and scratched at the tinted window.

The whole time Sam was quietly muttering to himself, or chuckling. I knew from experience that Sam was now officially lost in thought and there wasn't much point in trying to talk to him. When he became fascinated with something, no matter how minor, he'd study it with his complete attention. This wasn't bad; however, at the end of the trip he'd want to tell me everything he'd learned about our bus.

"Alex, what's that?" Sam asked.

"I don't know," I answered, looking where he was pointing. "It looks like some sort of screen or a TV."

"It *is* a TV," Twilight said. "At least a TV screen. They show movies."

"You're kidding, aren't you? I thought that was only on airplanes."

"On commuter buses, too. People spend a lot of time on these things and they want to be entertained," Twilight explained.

"Do you think they'll show something today?" Sam asked.

The words had hardly escaped his mouth when the screen flickered to life and a movie, partway through, came to life.

"That is so amazing!" Sam said. "Just so amazing!"

Twilight shook her head slowly and there was a sad

expression on her face. "You'd think the boy had never seen a movie before. You two really have to get out of Farmingdale more often."

I felt annoyed, as I always did when she insulted my town—and us. But for Sam it fell like water off a duck's back. I doubted he'd even heard her, and if he had he wouldn't have bothered to pay attention.

"But how do you listen?" Sam asked.

Twilight sighed and then reached into the armrest. "With these," she said, a pair of earphones dangling from her hand. She reached over and tossed them onto his lap.

Sam leaned forward, open-mouthed, and stared at the screen. It did seem as though this *was* the first movie he'd ever seen.

I turned to Twilight. She was looking out the window. I caught my own faint reflection glaring back at me in the glass. I'd temporarily forgotten I was a "girl." I glanced down at my soft blue sweater, and reached up to feel the wig on my head. I licked my lips and tasted the lipstick, Twilight's lipstick. It tasted just as I'd imagined it would, all tangy and sort of sweet and exotic. I licked my lips again. I had to admit, there had been times over the past weeks when I'd idly wondered what her lipstick might taste like . . .

"Interesting taste, isn't it?"

I was jarred back into reality and turned to see Twilight staring at me. "Ah, yeah . . . I guess so."

I was hit with one of those illogical and embarrassing thoughts, like maybe she hadn't just been watching me but reading my mind.

"You know, Alex, you're really pretty cute . . ." Twilight said.

I felt myself turning red and . . .

". . . for a girl!" She laughed.

"Gee, thanks," I answered sarcastically, trying to hide my embarrassment.

"You should take a stroll through the bus and see if there's anybody on board you know," Twilight suggested.

"Me? Why me?" I protested indignantly. The last thing in the world I wanted to do was parade around the bus looking like the losing contestant in the Junior Miss New Jersey beauty pageant.

"Well, Alex, it doesn't make sense for me to go since I don't know who you know or who might know you. And, judging from the look on Sammy's face, he's lost in the movie."

She had that right—Sam was mesmerized.

"Don't worry, Alex," Twilight continued. "You don't have to go. Especially if you like being dressed like a girl. Because until you check, you can't risk taking off the disguise. You'll have to stay dressed that way. I don't care myself. As far as I'm concerned you can spend the entire bus ride, even the entire weekend, dressed as a girl. I always wanted a sister. We can exchange girl talk, put make-up on each other, share clothes. It'll be great . . . Alexis."

I got up, cursing quietly to myself, straightened the wig and started up the aisle. I tried to move casually, but it was hard to keep my balance and look out of the corner of my eye at each passenger I passed. Slowly I kept on moving until I'd reached the front of the bus.

"Excuse me, how long until we reach New York?" I asked the driver in my best "girl" voice.

"About an hour and fifteen minutes," he answered.

"Thank you," I said, and started back to my seat.

There were twenty-three passengers on the bus. Twenty-three strangers. I sat back down and allowed myself the very first smile of the trip. After yanking off the wig, I pulled the sweater off over my head and rubbed the back of my hands against my cheeks and lips to remove the rouge and lipstick. Things were definitely looking up. I was still positive we'd get caught, but at least now I'd get caught as a boy.

Twilight had moved into my seat and I sat down in the empty seats in front, grabbing the window seat. It was nice being so high up and looking down on the surroundings. We weren't getting anywhere in a hurry because the bus had to stop to pick up packages or passengers in almost every town we passed. I enjoyed looking at the stores lining each main street, the trees with their fall colors and the people who strolled along the sidewalks. Between the towns were houses and farms and gravel pits and gas stations and restaurants. I liked traveling this route so much more than driving along the Garden State Parkway. I turned around and peeked over the seat. Sam was still lost in the movie.

I settled back into my seat. Just as I was starting to get drowsy, I realized that we were joining up with the interstate. Cars and trucks started to zoom by us. I should have figured that there was no way to enter New York City without having to hit a major highway, at least for a short distance, to go across the bridges or into a tunnel—after all, the most exciting part of the city was on a very crowded island. In our case, we were heading for the Lincoln Tunnel.

Looking up ahead, I saw the office towers of the city poke above the horizon—the Empire State Building, the Chrysler tower and all the others huddled together. I took a deep breath. This was really happening. The bus seemed to be drawn to the towers like metal filings to a magnet. There was no way to break free now.

The city continued to get bigger and bigger. Gigantic electronic signs lined the highway selling cars, cameras and computers in big flashing letters. One sign gave the time: 5:32. Another one displayed the thought for the day: "To travel hopefully is often a better thing than to arrive."

Oh great, just what I needed, a sign telling me what a bad idea this was.

The bus decelerated and we started down a ramp, but we were soon anchored in a sea of stopped vehicles. The bus lurched forward for a few seconds and then came to a stop again. This was repeated two more times before it finally kept moving and plunged into the tunnel.

The overhead lights glowed brightly. Above the lights, I knew, were hundreds of feet of dirt, topped by the Hudson River. The bus picked up speed and the walls of the tunnel blurred by us. Soon the road began to go up, which meant we'd passed the halfway mark and were headed back for the surface. The tunnel curved to the right. Curving, curving, curving until it felt as though we'd doubled back and were heading to New Jersey again. Up ahead I saw light. Light at the end of the tunnel. The bus shot out into it. We circled and took a tight curve and came out on the city streets.

We eased into the city traffic and came to a near standstill. All around us were cars and trucks and taxis and city buses. The cars were almost all new and expensive, and every one, without exception, held only one person, the driver. But none of these vehicles was traveling very quickly. People on the sidewalk moved exactly in pace with us. The only things moving fast were the bicycles, which raced into view, jockeyed in and around the people and vehicles and then vanished. I kept my eye on one as it zipped forward and saw what was slowing us down: construction up ahead had closed some of the lanes. The traffic from three lanes was funneling into one and the vehicles shuffled for position, honking their horns at each other. My father always said that there were only two seasons in New York: winter and road construction.

We squeezed through the construction and the road opened up again. We made two tight turns, and we rocked from side to side in our seats. The bus started down a long curving incline and we were underground again. There was a sign announcing that we were going under the bus station.

"Hey, what happened?" Sam asked. "The movie . . . it stopped."

"We're here," I said. I suddenly realized that Sam was still in his wig and fluffy pink sweater. He'd been so absorbed in the movie that he'd forgotten to take them off.

"But the movie wasn't over," Sam said.

"It's over for you," Twilight said.

The bus squealed to a stop alongside a whole row of other buses.

"Last stop, Port Authority Bus Terminal. Please take all your possessions with you as you disembark," came the driver's voice, crackling over the P.A. system.

I grabbed my backpack and Sam's while Twilight slung hers over her shoulder.

"Come on, Samantha, it's time to go," I said.

"Samantha?" Sam said. "What do you mean . . . ? Oh, that's right." A few long blond strands from his wig had swept across his face and jogged his memory. He pulled the wig off and handed it to Twilight, who stuffed it in her bag.

Twilight led the way back up the aisle. Everybody else had already left the bus. The driver had his head down, filling in some papers, but caught sight of Twilight out of the corner of his eye.

"Take care, girls. I hope you enjoyed your . . ." He looked up and saw Sam and me, and his words stuck in his throat.

"Thanks," Twilight replied as she left the bus. "This trip certainly changed *their* lives."

I bumped into Sam, who had stopped beside the driver, and practically pushed him down the steps. We hurried to catch up to Twilight.

Chapter Eight

There we were on a concrete island, one of many, amid a sea of asphalt crowded with buses. If you thought about it, in fact, the whole city of New York was one big concrete-and-asphalt island. Fumes flowed out of the buses' tailpipes. It smelled awful, and I was positive it would give me a sinus headache if I didn't get away fast. We followed the other passengers through a sliding door into the terminal. The walls were lined with gray and red tiles. Above each door leading back to the buses were signs announcing times and destinations. There were rows of seats that were more like places to lean than places to sit. When somebody stood up, the little narrow seat would swing upright. They didn't look too comfortable, but as soon as somebody left, two more people would rush forward to compete for the newly vacated perch.

The whole place reeked of diesel fumes, and each time the sliding doors opened to welcome in more passengers from the bus bays, a new wave of fumes wafted in. It left a bad taste in my mouth, sort of like the taste you get after you drink a diet soda.

I'd been to the airport a couple of times before, when we picked up my mother's aunt and when we went to Disney World. But I'd never been at a bus station. There were some things the same—people coming and going, hugging and crying and shaking hands. But here there was no fancy luggage or men in business suits with their briefcases or even families coming back from fancy holidays. The bus people looked younger and poorer, and the closest thing to matching luggage was a guy carrying his stuff in two identical shopping bags with "Filmore Groceries" printed on the sides.

A constant buzz of conversation filled the air. There was a burst of noise from the P.A. system but I couldn't understand anything except "Thank you" at the end of each message.

"Can we get out of here?" I asked, turning to my friends.

They were gone! In shock I scanned the crowd. A lady moved to one side and I saw Sam and Twilight, only a few feet away, consulting a map. I quickly moved to join them.

"Why are you looking at that?" I asked.

"Just checking," Twilight answered calmly, without raising her eyes.

"Checking what?" I asked anxiously.

"How to get from here to where we're going," she replied.

"You mean you don't know? I thought you knew your way around the city!" I yelled. A couple of people turned and looked at us.

"Keep your voice down, Alex. Try to stay calm. I do know my way around the city. It's just I didn't live here as long as I lived in Paris or London. I know my way around those two cities much better."

"Twilight, we're not in London or Paris. This is New York!" I said, my voice rising again.

"Thank you for that fascinating piece of information. We'd be totally lost without you, Alex, dear," she responded without taking her eyes off the map. "I'd know my way around better if my mother hadn't been so nervous about me being alone downtown. She always said it was too dangerous for an eleven-year-old."

"Quit joking around, Twilight, this isn't funny," I said.

Twilight looked up from the map, directly at me. "I'm not joking, Alex."

"What do you mean you're not joking?" I shouted. "What do you mean you hardly know your way around?

What do you mean your mother never left you alone downtown because it was too dangerous?"

"Alex, don't worry, I'm not alone now. I'm here with you and Sam. You don't see Sam getting all nervous and excited. Right, Sam? Sam . . . Sam . . . ?"

Sam wasn't there.

"Where is he?"

"I don't know," Twilight said casually. "He's always wandering off."

"He's always wandering off in Farmingdale. This is New York. Where is he?"

"He was here just a second ago. He couldn't have gone far. Maybe he went to ask at the counter if somebody could tell him how the movie ended." She was trying to sound calm but not succeeding.

Sam was nowhere to be seen. At the end of the waiting area there was a set of stairs leading to the surface. I threaded my way around people, Twilight right behind me, until we reached them, and I started up, two steps at a time.

"He can't be far ahead of us," Twilight said, puffing.

The stairs emptied into the main lobby. It had high ceilings and the air there wasn't contaminated by bus fumes. Stores lined one side and a big magazine stand was right in front of us. It was crowded, and people flowed around us as we stood there, peering around.

"Look!" I shouted, "There he is!"

Sam was moving in the direction of a side door. He was hardly visible among a group of older teenagers. I could only see a glimpse of him between them, and one of them was carrying his backpack!

"Hey!" Twilight yelled. Her voice was absorbed by the crowd and disappeared before it could reach Sam.

The group turned a corner and was gone. We raced across the marble floor, bumping into each other as we rounded the corner.

"Stop!" Twilight yelled.

One of the teenagers turned and gave a little smile, but they kept moving. They walked through a revolving door and left the building.

"Come on, we have to catch them!" I shouted.

I reached the door and Twilight smacked in behind me, in the same cramped section. We spun around and the door spat us out on the other side.

"Stop! Wait!" Twilight screamed.

This time they all stopped. Sam gave us a little wave.

We ran right up to the group. There were seven of them, five boys and two girls. They all towered over Sam and us. They were one mean-looking group. They were a lot older than we were, maybe seventeen or eighteen, or even older. Two of them had completely shaved heads. One of the baldies was a girl. The others had an assortment of spikes, shaved stripes and multi-colored rainbows streaking through whatever hair remained. Their clothes were almost all the same, as if they were wearing a uniform: heavy black laced boots, ripped and torn jeans, dirty T-shirts topped by green army fatigue jackets. Earrings, nose rings and tattoos were visible on most of them. One had about a dozen rings piercing an eyebrow, making it look like one of those spiral notepads. The rings hung down, partially blocking that eye.

"Where are you going with our friend?" Twilight demanded to know.

The largest member of the group stepped forward ominously. He was tall and skinny and his face was pocked with acne scars. He had a large studded nose ring bearing a swastika.

"We're just taking our new friend here for a little walk," he answered, trying to sound sincere. "Do you two want to come along?"

He looked like some sort of slimy snake dressed in human clothing. Up close, his yellow-toothed smile made him seem even more frightening.

"They were just going to show me the street we should take to get to Madison Square Garden," said Sam cheerfully. Trust Sam to trust a bunch of goons who looked as if they could strangle puppies. That was just so like him.

"That's right. We were just being helpful. I'm Skully," the skinny guy said, offering his hand.

"We don't need your help," Twilight said.

"Everybody needs help in a big city like this. Here, let me carry one of your bags," the bald girl said to us, and she reached out her hand.

I pulled my backpack closer to my body.

"No!" Twilight snapped back. "We don't need your help. All we need is for you to leave us alone. Sam, come on."

"Who do you think you are, his mother?" the Skully guy said menacingly. "He can come with us if he wants. If you two don't want to come along you can blow away," he spat out scornfully.

He took two steps toward us. I instinctively stepped back. Twilight didn't. I looked up at his face. There was a series of small tattoos, teardrops, that ran down his left eye to his cheek.

"Give him back his backpack, and then *you* better blow away," Twilight told him.

The teenagers smirked and laughed at her threat. I turned to Twilight, my mouth open, wondering how she could be that brave . . . or stupid.

"And if we don't?" Skully asked. "Are you going to make me? Are you going to hurt me? Or is your little friend here gonna beat me up?" He gestured to me.

"We can take care of ourselves, especially Alex," she said.

I looked at her in amazement and then turned to Skully and offered him a weak, apologetic smile.

"But we don't have to fight you," Twilight said calmly. "All I have to do is yell. In five seconds I'm going to start screaming at the top of my lungs, and I know the Transit Police will rush over here to investigate and they'll arrest you."

They all started laughing. Not a good sign, I thought.

"Gee, now that *is* scary," Skully replied while the others laughed even harder. "Maybe you ain't noticed, but you ain't inside the bus station no more."

For the first time I looked around us. We were on some sort of covered street. There was traffic rolling by us, but a roof over our heads. The far sidewalk was lined with garbage cans and cardboard boxes. As I watched, a woman climbed out of one of the boxes and stretched. A few other people shuffled along the sidewalk. One of them pushed a grocery cart overflowing with garbage.

The sidewalk on our side of the street was deserted. There was no garbage, and strangely the whole wall of the bus station was painted in soft blues and greens, to look like it was underwater; whales and dolphins "swam" past us. Somehow it all seemed right, because I felt like we were about to become fish food.

"Sam, how much money do you have in your backpack?" Twilight asked.

"I don't know . . . do you want me to check?" Sam asked.

"No, just make a guess," Twilight replied.

"Maybe fifty dollars or so," Sam answered.

"That's what I thought." She turned directly to Skully. "Is it worth getting arrested for fifty bucks?"

"Maybe not," he answered. "Is it worth getting *beat up* for that amount? Maybe not? Why don't you just let us walk away with the backpack and we'll keep the fifty."

"You can't have fifty, but you can have five," Twilight said.

"Five bucks?" the bald girl asked.

"No, like I said, five seconds." Twilight started counting, One . . . two . . ."

This wasn't working. Skully wasn't even looking at us. He was looking over our heads, past us, as if he wasn't even interested in Twilight's threat. I had three more seconds to live.

"Three . . . four . . ."

"Scatter!" Skully ordered.

All at once Sam's backpack dropped to the ground and the gang took off in different directions and disappeared, except for Skully, who hesitated a second longer.

"I'll see you three later. Count on it!" he snarled, and then he turned and ran back through the revolving door.

"What happened?" My heart was booming in my ears. I was wondering if this was what it felt like to have a heart attack.

"Bullies don't like a fight," she replied. "We showed them!"

"I just wish somebody had showed us the way to the Garden," Sam said. "Maybe one of those police officers can direct us." He pointed behind where Twilight and I stood. We turned around and saw two cops rapidly approaching. They were looking right at us. It all clicked. Skully must have seen them coming up behind us. Then another thought fell into place.

"It's all over," I said. "They're going to ask us where we're from and where our parents are and then that's the end of it."

"Maybe not," was Twilight's answer.

"There's no *maybe* about it, Twilight . . ."

"GRANDMOTHER!" Twilight yelled.

She dashed toward the two officers, brushed right between them and kept on running. The cops turned and watched her go. She ran along the empty sidewalk until she reached an older woman standing beside an elderly gentleman. Then she threw her arms around the woman and gave her a big hug.

"Wow, her grandmother's here!" Sam said in amazement.

"It's not her grandmother," I whispered. "Come on."

I grabbed Sam by the arm and hurried past the two officers. We stopped in front of Twilight and the two elderly people. Risking a glance backward, I saw that the two cops had turned away—they must have been satisfied that we were with our family.

"Young lady, please stop!" The elderly woman was clearly shocked. "I'm not your grandmother!"

Twilight released her grip and stepped back, looking totally confused. "You're not my grandmother . . . so I guess that means you're not my grandfather either?" For a second, I thought she was going to turn on the phony waterworks.

"No dear, I'm terribly sorry," the man apologized.

"No, it's me who should be sorry. It's just . . . I haven't seen my grandparents for so long, and I guess all old folks look the same to me," Twilight said.

She walked off quickly and Sam and I followed her. We turned the corner of the building. The street sign read Eighth Avenue.

Chapter Nine

We moved quickly along the sidewalk. I kept looking back nervously over my shoulder, afraid we were being followed by those punks. It was crowded and we were pushed and bumped and jostled by the crowd. Twilight moved ahead of us, and I grabbed Sam by the hand and pulled him along. We had to keep up. We couldn't afford to get separated. Twilight stepped out of the flow of people and into the alcove of a store. I towed Sam along until we reached her side.

"Sam, stay close," I cautioned him as I released his hand. "I don't want you talking to any more strangers."

"Strangers?" he questioned vacantly.

"Yes, strangers, like that Skully guy!" I said, incredulous.

"What did you think you were doing, taking off with him like that?"

"He was probably okay," Sam answered innocently, and I knew he meant it. Sam had never harmed anybody and couldn't believe anybody would harm him.

"Sam, listen to Alex," Twilight told him. "He was going to take your money and your stuff, maybe even hurt you."

"Really?"

"Really," I answered. "He and his friends could have killed you and your friends."

"Not necessarily," Twilight chipped in. "I can take care of myself, and there are the two of you. We could have put up a good fight."

Neither Sam nor I answered.

Twilight looked at us. "Right? We could have put up a fight?"

"I don't have much experience with fighting," I reluctantly admitted.

"Sam?" she asked.

"I've only been in one fight in my whole life," Sam replied.

"One?" Twilight asked. "How about you, Alex? How many fights have you been in before?"

"One," I said sheepishly.

"One? . . . Oh, let me guess . . ."

"That's right, we fought each other," I admitted.

Twilight started to laugh. "Who won?"

"Nobody," Sam answered. "We both lost."

"What do you mean, you both lost? Somebody had to win." Twilight wouldn't let it alone.

"Nope. We both hit each other and ran home to tell our mommies," Sam said.

"Mommies?"

"Yeah. What did you call *your* mother when you were five years old?" I asked.

"And that was it? One fight when you were five years old? Oh man, you two better stick really close to me for the rest of the weekend."

Twilight pulled out her map again. "We have to figure out how to get to my father's."

"Can I see it?" Sam asked.

"I'm the one who knows the city. I can find it," Twilight said defiantly.

"Are you sure?" I asked. "Sam's pretty good with things like maps."

She opened her mouth as though she was going to argue, then closed it again without saying a word and handed Sam the map.

Sam slumped to the sidewalk, unfolded the map and began studying it.

"Do you think he can find it?" Twilight whispered.

I nodded. "Maps are like plans, so Sam can do it."

"This is where we are," he said, pointing to a spot on

the map. "Eighth Avenue and West Forty-second Street. Where's your father's apartment?"

"It's not far . . . at least I don't think it's far . . . it's . . . it's down by Washington Square."

"That's right here," Sam said, pointing at the map. "What's the address?"

"I don't really know the address," she mumbled.

"What?"

"I don't really know the address. It's on West Fourth Street . . . I know the building . . . what it looks like."

"How can you not know the address where—?"

"West Fourth is right . . . here," Sam announced triumphantly, pointing once again to the map.

"How far away is that?" I asked, turning my attention away from Twilight and toward Sam.

"Looks like about three or four inches," Twilight said brightly.

I shot her a dirty look. "How far away is it, Sam?"

"Thirty-eight blocks."

"That's not close. How are we going to get there?"

"Subway. We'll take the subway," Twilight suggested.

"No way!" I shot back. "I'm not going into the subway in New York City. Don't you ever listen to the news? People get killed down there!"

"It's not that bad," Twilight scoffed. "Besides, how else will we get there?"

"We could walk," Sam offered.

"Thirty-eight blocks! No way I'm walking that, especially carrying this backpack," she objected. "That's out. Besides, in case you haven't noticed, the sun is starting to go down. Do you really think it would be safer to be on the streets after dark?"

I really didn't like the sound of that. "Well . . . how about taking a cab? Look at all the taxis!" I pointed out to the street. It seemed like almost every second vehicle was a bright yellow taxi.

"Good luck," Twilight countered.

"What do you mean?"

"It's Friday at rush hour. Do you really think we can get a cab?"

"Why not? There's enough of them."

"Yeah, and they're all taken. Look for yourself."

I scanned the taxis that were close by. She was right. Each vehicle held at least one passenger in the back seat.

"Besides, the taxis are hardly moving. It would cost us a small fortune to travel that far through rush-hour traffic," Twilight pointed out.

Again, I had to admit, at least to myself, that she had a good point. The cabs were barely inching forward. Nobody was going anywhere fast. One of the drivers suddenly lay on the horn at another, who responded by leaning out the window and yelling. I didn't understand what he was screaming but I was pretty sure it wasn't English.

"So we don't have a choice. We take the subway," Twilight decided. "And if you'd have listened to me in the first place instead of arguing, we'd be halfway there by now, Alex."

Sometimes she got me so angry I was speechless. My mind sputtered and fired blanks for a few seconds before I could talk. "How do you even know we can find a subway station? It isn't like they're on every corner, you know."

Twilight and Sam both broke out laughing. I stared at them angrily. Twilight pointed above our heads. We were standing beneath a sign: "SUBWAY."

"But if you don't like this entrance, we could cross the street and go in the one on the other corner." She pointed. "Or maybe the entrance on that corner? Say . . . it does look like there's a subway on every corner, doesn't it?"

Twilight picked up her backpack and started to walk toward the entrance. I remained frozen to the spot, too dispirited to even move.

"Come on, Alex," Sam said, patting me on the back. "Just go with the flow and don't worry." He walked after Twilight, who had now joined the rush of people streaming in through the entrance. There was no choice.

I threaded my way through the crowd and quickly caught up to Sam. He grabbed the door and swung it open. We were instantly hit with a blast of air. I hesitated for a split second and was bumped from behind, pushed along by the crowd. Up ahead Twilight looked back and waved. She was starting down an escalator. By the time I reached the top she was already at the bottom.

I turned to say something to Sam, but a woman stared back at me. Then I saw Sam's head bobbing up and down, jogging down the stairs beside the escalator. We both hit bottom together.

"Do you see Twilight?" I asked.

Before the last word was out of my mouth, I caught sight of her. She was standing by a turnstile. We reached her and stepped out of the stream of traffic flowing through the turnstiles. I heard the sound of a train swooping by and a blast of air quickly followed.

"Here, take these subway tokens," she offered.

"Where did you get them?" Sam asked.

"From a machine. Let's go."

She dropped the token in a slot and pushed through the bar. We did the same and caught up to her once again.

"Do you know where we're going?" I asked.

"Not exactly. Maybe we can ask somebody. Look! There's an information booth."

There was a man sitting in a booth. He was completely enclosed in steel and glass. We stopped in front of him.

"Can you tell us how to get to Washington Square?" Twilight asked.

A garbled electronic-sounding voice came back through the speaker.

"Did you understand what he said?" Twilight asked.

Sam and I shook our heads. She asked him again. He gave an angry glare and then barked out his reply. Twilight, Sam and I exchanged puzzled glances.

"Did you understand him that time?"

"I caught some of it," I replied. "Something about two floors down and take a train."

"That's very helpful . . . 'take a train.' What did he figure we were going to take, an airplane?" Twilight snapped.

I looked over at Sam. He had a map in his hand, but not Twilight's map.

"What's that?" I asked him.

"A subway map. They're on the ledge of the booth," Sam answered without looking up.

Right now I was really grateful that my best friend was a weird kind of genius. His brain was aimed at finding the apartment, and nothing else—the noise, the people rushing by, the flashing signs—was going to distract him. He would get us where we were going, as long as I made sure he didn't fall in front of a train.

Sam started walking slowly. He looked first at the map and then at the overhead signs and then back at the map. He bumped into a large man carrying a briefcase. I apologized for him because I didn't think Sam even noticed. We walked down two flights of stairs and came to a crowded platform with train tracks on both sides.

"Is this it? Is this where we catch the train?" Twilight asked.

"This is definitely the place," Sam answered. "I'm just not sure which train we catch."

"Where you kids trying to get to?" The voice came from behind us. I turned around. It was a woman.

"Um . . . Washington Square," Sam answered.

So much for not talking to strangers. At least this one was a well-dressed woman with a briefcase, and nothing pierced but her ears.

"You're on the right platform. Now all you have to do is get on the right train," she offered. "Different trains use these same tracks. Some are express trains. They may stop here but they don't stop again until they hit Rockaway Park."

"Is that far?"

"Far! That's hardly in New York any more. You'd be all the way on the other side of Jamaica Bay."

"That wouldn't be good, would it?" I ventured.

"Not good, for sure. You want to make sure you get on a local train."

"How can we tell a local train?"

"Look at the front of the train. There'll be a sign. It'll either say local or express. Make sure it isn't an express. Understand?"

In the distance I heard a train coming. The noise grew loud quickly and ruled out any more questions. A light appeared in the tunnel and then the train burst into the station, and the breaks squealed to a stop.

"This is an express. I'm getting on this one," the woman said. The doors opened and she stepped on, waving goodbye.

As the first train pulled out of the station, another train, on the tracks on the other side of us, came roaring in. I looked up in time to see the sign on the front: it said Local 8.

"Local!" I yelled over the noise of it shrieking to a stop. Both Twilight and Sam nodded in agreement.

The doors opened and people spilled out onto the platform. As the last ones scrambled off, we rushed through the doors. People crowded in all around me. The doors closed and the train started rolling. I stumbled and grabbed on to a pole. Twilight started to snicker.

"Next time maybe I can fall flat on my face and give you a real belly laugh," I suggested.

"That would be nice," she answered.

Sam was still holding the map and ignoring me,

Twilight and everybody else in the crowded train.

"It's cool in here!" Twilight announced. She was right. I could feel a stream of fresh air on my face.

"The trains are air-conditioned," a woman standing beside Twilight said.

"A lot better than it used to be!" another woman added.

"You can say that again!" a man interjected. "It was like being in a steam bath riding the subway in the summer. I don't miss it at all."

"You kids know where you're going?" the first woman asked.

"Sort of," I answered hesitantly.

"'Sort of' isn't good in New York," she responded.

"Washington Square station," Twilight said.

"You can definitely get there from here. Fourth stop."

I felt a surge of relief. I had faith in Sam, but it was good to hear it from somebody else.

"Where are you kids from?" a man asked.

"Um . . . New Jersey," I replied. "But how did you know we weren't from here?"

"Come on, kid, the only thing missing is 'I LOVE N.Y.' T-shirts. He's holding a map, and you all look lost. You three practically got the word 'tourist' stamped on your foreheads." He laughed.

I felt the train start to decelerate as we came into a

station. I looked at the sign on the wall: Thirty-fourth Street, Penn Station.

"Three more stops," Sam said.

The doors opened and we got off the subway train. We were at Washington Square. As we stood on the platform, I turned back to the car and watched the doors close. Two of the people we'd been talking to looked out the window and waved goodbye. The train started up again and disappeared into the tunnel.

"Everybody was very friendly," Sam commented.

"Yeah . . . not like I think of New York. Everybody's supposed to be mean. At least that's what it's like on TV," I replied.

"Yeah, and there's supposed to be garbage all over, and the subway cars should be covered with graffiti," Sam added.

"That's all just TV. This is real life," Twilight interjected. "It's just like Farmingdale except bigger. A lot bigger."

We pushed through a set of heavy doors and were out on the street. It was dark; night had come while we were underground. But one thing was the same—the road was filled with honking taxis. In the distance I heard the wail of a police car. I had an uneasy feeling. People rushed by on the sidewalk and it was hard to avoid being shoved along with them. Up ahead a man stood on the sidewalk playing the saxophone; people were tossing loose change into his open case. People moving along the sidewalk shifted to either side as a woman came toward us pushing a shopping cart overloaded with junk. She was yelling and screaming. She wasn't making any sense at all, and I couldn't figure out why she was so mad. I scrunched as far as I could to the edge of the sidewalk to let her pass by and watched her until she was swallowed up by the crowd once again.

I turned to Twilight. "Just like Farmingdale?"

"Maybe not exactly."

"I think I want to get off the street as soon as possible. How far is it from here?" I asked.

"About that far," Twilight said, pointing to a building just up the block. "Race you there!"

Twilight took off. Sam and I charged after her, dodging between the people on the crowded sidewalk. She ran up the front stairs of the building and we followed after her. At the top there was a fancy-looking intercom system and a big, heavy security door. Twilight grabbed at the door and pulled it. It opened.

"Some security system," she noted.

We entered the lobby.

"Stairs. Where are the stairs?" Sam asked.

"I don't know anything about any stairs. The elevators are over there." Twilight pointed.

"Good. The stairs are usually close to the elevators," Sam said.

"Why are we looking for stairs?" Twilight asked.

"I want to take the stairs," Sam answered, looking down at his shoes.

"Do you realize my father lives in apartment eighteen-ten, and the eighteen means that the apartment is on the eighteenth floor . . . the top floor?" Twilight asked.

Sam nodded.

I tapped Sam on the shoulder and he looked at me. "I don't like elevators," he said quietly.

"You'd better learn to like them, unless you want to walk up eighteen flights," Twilight told him.

I shushed her. "Sam . . . are you afraid of elevators?"

He nodded ever so slightly.

"I didn't know."

"It doesn't come up much in Farmingdale," he replied.

"You're right about that." I chuckled. "It's like being afraid of alligators. There are none of those in town, either. Where are the stairs?"

Sam smiled brightly.

Twilight scowled. "You're both nuts! You two can have a lovely little hike and I'll meet you at the top." She stomped away to the elevators.

Sam pointed to a red exit sign just off to the side of the lobby.

"Have a nice climb!" Twilight yelled to us as she poked the Up button.

We pushed through the door into the stairwell. As it shut behind us, I heard the *ping* of the elevator arriving. We started to climb. I counted the stairs: one, two, three, four, five, six, seven, eight, nine, ten and then a landing. Up the next flight of ten stairs to reach the second floor. A large door with a big number 2 on the back.

I heard a door open below us. "Hey, wait up!" Twilight called out.

We stopped, and Sam and I exchanged smiles. Twilight bounded into view, two steps at a time. She was slightly out of breath when she reached us.

"Good to see you," I said.

"No problem. Anyway, I figured you two might get lost without me."

Twilight ran up the next few steps, leaving us on the landing behind her. "We've only got sixteen more stories to go. By the way—" she kept on climbing "—last one up fixes breakfast in the morning!" She raced off, turned the corner of the landing and disappeared from sight. Sam and I bumped into each other as we raced after her.

We dragged ourselves up the last flight of stairs. Somewhere around the twelfth floor, Sam and I had realized that we had no chance of catching Twilight. I'd been panting so hard I had to stop and pull my puffer out of my backpack. We agreed to tie for last place and fix breakfast together.

We turned the final corner and climbed the final flight of stairs. Twilight was sitting on the floor, her back against the door with the number 18 painted on it, a look of smug satisfaction on her face. She pulled open the door and bowed gracefully. We entered the carpeted hallway and stopped—which way should we go? Twilight took the lead and we followed her to an apartment door.

"Eighteen-ten. This is it," she announced.

She removed a key from her pocket, eased it into the lock and gently turned it. The door swung open, and light from the hall haloed into the darkened apartment.

"I'm glad that worked," Twilight said with obvious relief.

"What do you mean, you're glad it worked?" I said.

"I've never used my key. My father only moved here after the separation, and it isn't like I'm here very often—and never by myself to open the door."

"And just what were we going to do if the key didn't work?" I asked, exasperated.

"Isn't that a little obvious . . . even to you?" she said as she took a step into the dark apartment.

"No!" I protested. "It isn't obvious to me!"

"If the key hadn't opened the door, then we would have slept—"

"Somewhere else," Sam interrupted.

"Exactly!" Twilight beamed.

I just shook my head in disgust. "Now I'm even more worried. The two of you are starting to think alike."

Twilight flicked on a light and the whole room brightened up. The wooden floors were made with gleaming parquet tiles, covered in a couple of places with expensive-looking carpets. Two big, overstuffed couches were the only furniture in the room. Everywhere there were boxes—little boxes, big boxes, sealed boxes, boxes with tissue paper hanging out, empty boxes—arranged in piles around the room. Leaning against the walls were pictures, waiting patiently to be hung.

"That's my father for you. Living out of a box or a suitcase is his style. If we come back again a year from now he still won't have unpacked everything," Twilight remarked.

Twilight and Sam spread out into the apartment, and I turned around and closed the door. I clicked the lock and put the chain on, as well.

"If anybody needs to use the bathroom it's right there." Twilight pointed to a darkened room.

She turned on the light in another room. "Here's the bedroom. One big, unmade bed!" she bellowed. "I don't think my father knows how to make a bed."

She flicked on another light—the kitchen—and walked in. I followed after her. She opened the fridge.

"Looks like 'Old Mother Hubbard.' Nothing here except for an empty carton of orange juice." She picked it up and turned it upside down. "And a lump of fuzzy greenish stuff growing in the milk. Anybody thirsty?" she asked, offering the green milk.

I had to work hard not to gag.

Sam opened cupboards. There were two boxes of cereal. He pulled them out and put them on the counter.

"I told you he wouldn't have much food," Twilight said.

"Or furniture or a TV or a stereo or—"

Twilight interrupted. "We get the idea, Alex."

"Except for the bed and the couches it's not so different from the stairwell," I noted sarcastically.

"At least it doesn't smell like the stairs," Sam remarked.

"Wow, you have a point there. The stairs smelled like somebody died in there," I agreed.

"More likely somebody *lived* there," Twilight said.

"Lived there?" Sam asked.

"Yeah, lived there. Street kids like your buddy Skully and his gang sometimes sleep in stairwells when the weather is bad."

"You're kidding," I said.

"No, I'm not. At least it's dry and out of the wind."

I looked around the apartment. "Suddenly this place doesn't look so bad any more."

Chapter Ten

There was an explosion of sound—a banging—and I sat bolt upright in bed. Just as suddenly it stopped. My eyes opened wide as they tried to adjust to the darkness of the room. What was that sound? Where had it come from? I listened intently.

The only light was a faint trickle coming around the edges of the partially closed door to the en-suite bathroom. I looked down at Sam. He was still asleep beside me. His chest went up and down, his mouth slightly open. A little bit of drool hung out of his mouth and glistened in the light.

The apartment was quiet. I settled back down on the mattress and closed my eyes. Whatever it was it was gone and—*BANG . . . BANG!* I jumped again. It sounded like somebody pounding on the door.

I glanced at the clock, which sat on top of a cardboard packing box. The time glowed back at me: 3:14 a.m. Quietly I rolled off the edge of the bed and scrambled on all fours into the living room. Almost immediately I bumped into Twilight, huddled behind the couch. The pounding came again, this time even louder. We exchanged looks and waited wordlessly. Thirty seconds passed, then another thirty and another. I felt my shoulders ease down. It looked like whoever it was had gone away.

Then I heard another noise: the unmistakable sound of keys, first just jingling together and then tapping against the door and the lock as they were pushed into place. Even in the darkness of the apartment I saw Twilight's eyes widen. I heard the lock click and the door started to open, letting in a shaft of light from the hallway until— *CRASH*—the chain lock stopped the door from opening more than two inches. I edged over, closer to Twilight.

"Brice . . . Brice . . . come on and open the door."

It was a woman's voice. It was soft and sweet and convincing.

"Come on, Brice, I know you can hear me. Let me in, *pleeaasse?*" she whined.

I placed my mouth against Twilight's ear. "Who is it?" I whispered.

She shrugged her shoulders in reply.

"Come on, Brice, let me in. It was a stupid fight. Isn't two weeks long enough for us to be mad at each other?" the woman asked in that same soft, pleading voice.

I didn't dare move or breathe.

"Bricey . . . come on . . . let me in. We'll talk about it until everything is right. Let me in. We can make it right."

Twilight moaned. "Bricey!" she whispered. "I think I'm going to be sick! He's got all these awful women who follow him around. I think they're really in love with Rex Ryan from the show, but they won't leave Dad alone. My mother really couldn't take it."

"Brice McKinnon!" the woman yelled through the opening, and I jumped, surprised by the sudden change in the tone of her voice. "I hear you mumbling away in there and I *demand* that you talk to me!"

"I'll talk to her," Twilight whispered fiercely. "I'll go and spit in her eye!" She started to get up.

I grabbed her arm and pulled her back down beside me. "What are you doing? Are you crazy?"

"I'm going to . . . I don't know what I was going to do," she admitted quietly.

"You know I always get what I want, Brice, and I want to talk to you. I'm not going away until you let me in and we talk," the woman threatened. "You know I'm stubborn enough to stay here all night if I need to. Unless you plan on jumping off the balcony there's no other way out!"

She was certainly right about that. Prior to going to bed I'd checked all the fire routes, and the balcony was the only other way out. If there had been a fire we could have waited out there for help, but there was no help coming for this. I was struck by the thought that we might have to stay right where we were, behind the couch, for the rest of the night, maybe the rest of the weekend. I couldn't go that long without food and water . . . or going to the bathroom. At that instant I realized I *did* have to go to the bathroom. Wetting my pants was not one of the new experiences I was hoping to have that weekend.

"Do you think she's faking the threat?" I asked.

"I don't think so."

"Do you think she'll go away soon?

"I don't think so," Twilight repeated.

"What are we going to do?" I asked, trying to hide the desperation in my voice.

"*We* are not going to do anything, Alex. You stay put and I'm going to try something," she whispered.

Twilight quietly crawled away, hidden behind the boxes and darkness. She moved slowly, around the outside of the room, until she was right behind the partially open door. I held my breath. Suddenly she stood up and slapped her hand against the door. I jumped as the woman yelped in shock.

"Get away and go home! Brice doesn't want to see you!"

It was definitely Twilight's voice but she sounded older.

"How rude of you to come here and disturb Brice and me in the middle of the night. It's no wonder he doesn't want to see you," Twilight continued, still out of sight behind the door.

The woman, who had probably been scared half to death by the slam on the door, recovered her senses enough to talk. "Who are you, and where is Brice?" she asked.

"Who I am is none of your business. I know who *you* are, and Brice doesn't want to talk to you," Twilight answered, her pretend-adult voice fading a bit as she spoke.

"I want to talk to Brice!" the woman demanded.

"He doesn't want to talk to you," Twilight repeated.

There was silence for a few seconds. Then, a bit louder, "She sounds awful young to me, Brice. Are you robbing the cradle now?" she asked, probably trying to provoke Brice into answering.

"You're right there," Twilight answered. "Compared to somebody as old as you, I'm practically a kid," she taunted.

"Fine, dearie," the woman said. "I'll wait until I can talk to you, too. I'm not leaving until Brice comes to the door."

"Brice is not coming. But the police are. We called

them a few minutes ago. It's your choice: leave now before they arrive or leave with them when they charge you," Twilight bluffed.

"You can't threaten me. I'm not afraid of the police," the woman said defiantly.

"Hah!" Twilight laughed. "You may be old but you're not very wise. Do me a favor and *don't* go away. Stay right here until the police come. I'd actually give up a night's sleep to have you arrested . . . Isn't there a clause in your contract about criminal charges and proper behavior? You'll probably lose your job and another actress—perhaps even *myself*—will take it."

There was silence.

"Now good night!" Twilight shouted as she slammed the door closed and turned the lock.

We waited together, in silence, separated by the darkness. Seconds passed. Twilight pressed her ear against the door and then jumped up into the air, pumped her arm and quietly mouthed the word "YESSSS!"

I jumped up from my hiding place and Twilight ran across the room. We met in the middle and threw our arms around each other. Then, like a bolt of lightning searing into my brain, I realized we were hugging. I released my grip, and she did likewise. We both turned away. I was grateful for the darkness so she couldn't see I was blushing. I swallowed hard before speaking.

"How did you know she was an actress?"

"Just a guess. Didn't you notice how she talked, the way she changed her voice?"

Of course Twilight was right. "Boy, will she be mad at your father."

"Good! That's what I want! I want her to be so mad she'll never talk to him again."

"But what will happen if she does call him and talk about tonight?" I asked.

Twilight laughed out loud. "I wish I could be there if she tries. I can just imagine the conversation. They'll both think the other is either crazy or a liar—which actually describes half the actors I've ever met."

"You're right," I agreed. "We'd better get back to sleep."

Twilight padded away into the second bedroom. I went back into my room, where Sam was gently snoring away. I was just going to climb in beside him when I remembered something. First I went to the bathroom. Then I went to the front door and checked the locks.

I pulled the blanket over my head to hide from the brightness. It was too early to get up. Snuggling down, trying to sink my head in the pillow, I felt warm and fuzzy and just wanted to stay in my bed . . . my bed? I opened my eyes and was jarred out of my peaceful sleep by the realization that I wasn't where I should be. This wasn't my bed. This wasn't my bedroom. This wasn't my house. This wasn't even my town. I thought about my parents, probably in the kitchen, sitting at the table, reading the newspaper. And when I went downstairs my mother would ask what I wanted for breakfast and—there was no point in thinking about any of that.

I was alone. I could hear Sam's voice, coming from the other room. I threw off the covers and climbed out of bed. Then I caught a glimpse of my reflection in a full-length mirror that leaned against the wall. Somehow, standing there in my Spider-Man pajamas, with my hair sticking up in twelve different directions, I didn't feel like a big-time adventurer. I licked the palm of my hand and ran it over my hair. That didn't help. Now I not only *looked* stupid, I *felt* stupid. I couldn't hide the hair but I could change out of the PJs before Twilight got a good look at them. I hoped she hadn't noticed last night.

"Good morning. I was just coming in to wake you up," Twilight said, leaning against the doorway.

I turned around and felt myself shudder. How long had she been there, watching?

"I'm up."

"I can see. Come for breakfast. Maybe we can find you some dead flies."

"Flies?" What was she talking about now?

"Yes, isn't that what the amazing Spider-Man eats for breakfast?" She laughed.

"Rice Krispies will do fine," I answered coldly, trying

to ignore her zinger. "But I thought we were supposed to fix you breakfast."

"Sam already did."

"I'll be there in a minute," I said.

Twilight walked away and I went into the bathroom and closed the door. Without my humidifier on all night my sinuses had sealed up as solid as cement. I blew my nose with a mighty honk. It helped a little. I did it again and again. There was a knock on the door.

"Alex, are you okay?" Twilight asked.

"Yeah. Why?"

"With all that honking it sounded like a flock of geese were in there with you, and I was afraid they were nibbling on your superhero jammies."

I opened the door. Twilight stood there smirking. I walked past her to the kitchen. She followed behind me making honking sounds.

I found Sam standing at the kitchen counter eating a heaping bowl of cereal—dry cereal. I guess that made more sense than pouring green milk on it. If only we'd had some ham . . . green milk and ham. That would have made Dr. Seuss proud!

"Alex, Twilight's been trying to convince me there was some lady who almost broke in here last night, and that I slept through the whole thing."

"Tell him, Alex. He doesn't believe me!" Twilight urged.

I turned directly to Sam. "Do you think she's trying to trick you, Sam?"

"Yes. She thinks I'm a country bumpkin."

"Tell him I'm not lying," Twilight said even more anxiously.

I smiled. "Okay . . . Sam, you're too smart for her. I don't know what she's talking about, and I'm disappointed Twilight would even ask me to lie to my best friend in the whole wide world."

Twilight's mouth dropped open with disbelief as Sam gloated. I gave Twilight my best smile. "That'll teach you to mess around with the incredible Spider-Man."

I poured myself a bowl of cereal and rummaged around for a spoon. There weren't any.

"You'll either have to wait until Sam is finished or use a fork," Twilight suggested. "My dad only has one spoon."

"You're not kidding, are you?"

She shook her head and handed me a fork. I started forking the cereal into my mouth. It crunched loudly. Dry and slightly stale. What a combination. This was not the breakfast of champions.

"Where should we go first today?" Twilight asked. "I was thinking the Statue of Liberty for sure, and the Central Park Zoo and—"

"Wait just a minute!" I sputtered, and a few pieces of cereal shot out of my mouth. "What are you talking about? We're not going anywhere except the concert."

"Alex, the concert doesn't start for another twelve hours. What do you expect us to do all day, stay in here and watch TV?"

"Sounds like a good plan to me." As far as I could tell this was the safest place in all of New York—sitting on the couch behind a locked door.

"No TV . . . remember?" Twilight said.

"Oh, yeah," I replied, feeling deflated.

"Besides, we can't waste this opportunity. We're in New York . . . the Big Apple . . . the center of the universe . . . on our own, and we can do anything we want, see anything we want. This is the chance of a lifetime!"

"We can't just wander all over New York. This place is huge and confusing. What makes you think we could even find our way around?" I asked her.

"We found our way here, didn't we? I just figure we stick a map under Sam's nose and follow him. Right, Sam?"

"For sure," he answered confidently.

I knew he could get us around, so there was no point in arguing. "I just think it would be safer to stay right here," I replied.

"I'm not so sure," Twilight shot back. "What about the middle-of-the-night lady?"

"Do you think she'd come back?"

"Come back? But you said there wasn't any—" Sam started to say.

"I lied," I admitted. "Do you really think she'd come back?"

"Maybe. Maybe not. How about a compromise?" Twilight asked.

"What do you mean, compromise?"

"Oh, I don't know," she answered innocently. "We could go out . . . for part of the day, and then come back here."

"How long would we be gone? When would we get back?"

"I don't know. In the afternoon . . . maybe late afternoon," she replied. "I'd even be willing to come back earlier if we had something to do . . . like, something to get us ready for the concert."

"Get ready how?" I asked.

"Oh, we'll figure that out later. Right now we need to decide where we're going to go. What about if we start at the Statue of Liberty or the Empire State Building?"

"We're not going to the Empire State Building," Sam said. "No way."

"Oh, yeah, that's right, you don't want to go in any elevators. Then how about we take the ferry over to the Statue of Liberty?"

"Sounds fantastic!" Sam agreed.

They both looked at me. I didn't even crack a smile. "Alex?" she asked.

"Fine. We'll go to the Statue of Liberty."

They both cheered wildly, and I couldn't stop myself from smiling.

Chapter Eleven

The taxi stopped directly in front of a building with a sign that read "Ferries." Twilight handed the driver a ten-dollar bill and told him to keep the change, and we climbed out.

"That certainly beats the heck out of taking the subway," I said.

"Taxis are good. Limos are better. Now let's hurry up or we'll miss the next ferry over to the Statue!" Twilight said.

She raced off, leaving Sam and me to scramble after her. We caught her in the line waiting to board.

The ferry looked big tied to the dock but awfully small compared with New York Harbor. It was being bounced around by the waves and repeatedly thumped heavily against the dock. The gangplank, which gently sloped down, rocked wildly. It was funny; it was clear and sunny and there was hardly any wind, but there were waves on the water.

I tried to angle myself into the middle of the shuffling crowd so I could walk down the center of the gangplank. As we stepped on, I felt my feet start to go out from under me and grabbed the railing to steady myself. I looked down into the water through the small gap between the ferry and dock. At that instant the boat was thrown against the dock and the strip of water disappeared. I shuddered to think what would happen to somebody who fell off the gangplank and into that space. He'd be crushed like a nut.

The crowd propelled me forward onto the boat. It rolled and I bumped against the woman beside me. I apologized and stumbled up the stairs. Twilight had already disappeared from view and Sam was following close behind. I jostled and shoved my way through the crowd. Reaching the top of the stairs, I saw the backside of Sam moving up another flight of stairs. I pushed up after him and came to the top deck. Sam and Twilight stood side by side at the front railing. I moved along the aisle between the benches and came up behind them. Just when I got there, the boat pitched forward and I stumbled into Twilight.

"Can we sit down?" I asked.

"Not me," Twilight replied. "I want to stay right here where I can see everything."

"I can see what I need to from the bench," I answered. I stepped back and squeezed into a space among a bunch of Japanese tourists. I looked down the bench, first in one direction and then the other. They were all wearing identical "I LOVE N.Y." T-shirts and had cameras dangling around their necks.

The ferry lurched violently to one side and my stomach became queasy in protest. I was struck by an awful thought. Right there, on the ferry over to the Statue of Liberty, I was going to hurl my breakfast. I could just picture it sloshing along the deck, back and forth with each roll of the boat, and all the tourists having one more memorable moment to capture with their cameras. Maybe I'd feel better if I stood with Sam and Twilight by the railing.

I jumped up and pushed between them. My stomach was doing flips and a small burp escaped. I looked over at Twilight and she shot me a look of total disbelief.

"Come on, Alex, not even you could get seasick on a five-minute ferry ride."

"I'm not seasick!" I lied.

"You do look a little green," Sam interjected.

"A little! He's as green as the Statue!"

"You're both crazy!" I snapped. "It's just the sun

reflecting off the green water. You both look green to me as well."

Twilight and Sam considered each other quizzically. Sam looked down at his arms and hands, turning them over as if he was examining a science experiment. "You're wrong, Alex. Twilight and I look fine. It's just you."

The ship rolled and my stomach sent up another cloud of gas, making me burp again. "I feel fine!" I protested.

"But you look—" Sam started to say.

"Leave him alone, Sam. If he says he's fine, he's fine," Twilight interrupted.

I wanted to thank her but stopped when I caught sight of a little smirk starting to grow on her face.

"I'm *sure* Alex is just fine," she said again. And she started swaying back and forth, exaggerating the motion of the ship. "All this rocking and rolling and bouncing doesn't bother him in the least . . . and he doesn't feel all warm and dizzy . . . and his head isn't fuzzy . . . and his stomach isn't all queasy like maybe he's going to hurl his breakfast right here on the deck of the—"

"Stop! Please stop!" I gagged. I hung my head over the railing and looked down at the murky green water.

"What's wrong, Alex, feeling a little bit sick?" Twilight taunted me.

I nodded in agreement but almost instantly regretted it.

The motion of my head only added to the motion of the ferry. I tried to focus my attention on Liberty Island, coming closer with each passing second. I needed to get off that boat and onto land—solid, unmoving, unrolling land.

The ferry came in close to the dock and two men tossed lines to sailors waiting ashore. They wrapped the ropes around gigantic pylons and secured us to the dock. The gangplank was lowered and the boat began to disgorge passengers. The crowd oozed along the dock and past a long line of people waiting to board the ferry.

"You okay, Alex?" Sam asked.

"I guess," I replied feebly.

"We'd better get off before they start letting people on."

Unsteadily I followed after them across the deck and down the two flights of stairs. I felt an incredible sense of relief when I crossed the gangplank and touched down on the concrete dock.

"Is that better?" Twilight asked. This time she sounded genuinely concerned.

"It will be . . . in a minute. It feels like the island is moving. Can we just sit down?" I asked.

We walked over to a bench. The tail end of the stream of people flowed off the ferry and walked in the direction of the Statue of Liberty.

"Just once I'd like to visit this thing without getting nauseous," I said quietly.

"You mean you've been here before?" Twilight asked, clearly amazed.

"Three times. Three times I've visited Liberty and three times I've gotten sick," I admitted.

"I can't believe it," Twilight said.

"It's not my fault. I just have a sensitive stomach, that's all."

"No, I don't mean the part about you getting sick all the time—that I believe. I mean the part about you having been here three times before."

"Why wouldn't you believe that?" I asked her.

"I've never actually met anybody who's been here that many times," Twilight answered.

"This is my seventh time," Sam added.

"Seven! You're joking, aren't you?"

"No. How many times have you been here?" I asked.

"Never."

"Never? You lived in New York City and you've never seen the Statue of Liberty before?"

"Of course I've *seen* it before, Alex. Hundreds and hundreds of times I've seen it from a distance. It's just that I've never come over on the ferry to see it in person."

"Why not?" Sam asked.

"My mother and father always said things like the Statue of Liberty were just for tourists. *Real* New Yorkers don't visit the tourist attractions," Twilight said with disdain.

"But these places are important. The Statue of Liberty is, like, the best-known sculpture in the world," Sam objected.

"Sculpture? You're lucky my mother isn't here," Twilight argued.

"But your mother's a sculptor. She should *love* this place," Sam reasoned.

"That's one of the reasons she detests this place in particular. She says it isn't a sculpture. It's a big, ugly, green building shaped like a lady," Twilight explained. "People don't walk around inside a sculpture."

"I'm confused," I said. "If it's just a big, ugly . . . green building . . . that's . . ."

"Shaped like a lady," Sam continued. "And real New Yorkers don't go to places like this . . ."

"Yeah, and real New Yorkers don't go to places like this, then why did *you* suggest we come here?" I asked Twilight.

"Because . . . because . . ."

I'd never seen Twilight at a loss for words. She always had something to say, even when she had nothing to say. I started to laugh.

"Oh, shut up! I guess this shows you what living in Farmingdale has done to me. After four weeks I've become a hick!" Twilight jumped to her feet and smiled. "Come on—are you ready to get going, Alex?"

"I'll be okay in another minute," I answered.

"I've sat long enough. I'm going to see what's inside that building. Maybe I can get something to eat," Twilight suggested.

The thought of food made me gag.

"I'm coming too," Sam announced, and he bounded to his feet.

I watched them weave in and out of the crowd moving across the square until they vanished into the tourist center.

I stayed seated and looked at the people filling the square, listening to little snippets of conversation as they filed past me. It seemed as though more than half of the people passing were speaking different languages, and even those speaking English seemed to have accents, as if they were from someplace else. I would never admit it to Twilight, but there probably was almost nobody here who actually lived in New York City.

My stomach was starting to feel a little better. A drink of water, to rinse out my mouth, would help. I got to my feet and started after Sam and Twilight. I climbed the steps and entered the building. Straight ahead were the restrooms. Off to one side was a snack bar and to the other a gigantic souvenir store. They were probably getting something to eat. I figured I could use a Coke, so I turned in to the snack bar.

There were big plastic tables with plastic chairs attached. A crowd was gathered at the counter ordering food. I scanned the crowd but couldn't see either of them. They had to be there somewhere. I walked into the center of the room and carefully looked in all directions. Even if I couldn't see them, I figured that they should be able to see me. Maybe they were in the restroom instead. Just as I left the snack bar I caught sight of Twilight. She was coming out of the souvenir shop, carrying a bag and something else in her hand. Sam walked beside her. He was wearing an I LOVE N.Y. T-shirt, and he had a bag tucked under his arm and a silly grin plastered across his face.

"Wanna see the great stuff I got?" Sam asked excitedly.

Before I could answer, he started to pull things out of the bag. He handed me a little Liberty statue, identical to one that Twilight was holding. Next he pulled out a small plastic globe; he shook it and a snowstorm engulfed another tiny statue. Sam pressed it into my hand. Next from the bag was a cardboard mask of Liberty. Sam held it to his face.

"Isn't it neat? I thought it would make a great Halloween costume or something. I even got one for you!" He reached into the bag, pulled out another mask and handed it to me.

"What do you think?" Sam asked.

"I . . . I just don't know what to say. Twilight . . ." I turned to where she had been standing, but she was gone. "Twilight?"

"She's over there," Sam said. "By the mailbox."

Twilight dropped something into the mail slot and the trotted back to join us.

"Nice stuff, Sam. Way cool," Twilight said.

"Thanks."

"What were you doing at the mailbox?" I asked.

"What do you think I was doing? I was mailing a postcard."

"You were what?"

"Mailing a postcard. If you send something from here it gets a special postmark from Liberty Island," she answered.

"But we can't let anybody know we're here!" I protested. "You can't just go and mail people postcards."

"Alex, I didn't mail postcards, just one postcard . . . to my mother."

"Your mother?"

"But your mother hates the Statue of Liberty," Sam reminded her.

"I know." She smiled. "And I'm going to insist on putting it front and center on the fridge . . . for a long time. Maybe you should send your parents a postcard too."

"I guess you're right. My parents might expect something like that. But will your mother?"

"Why wouldn't she?"

"Because you said your parents—*both* your parents— would never go to places like this, so how are you going to explain being here with your father?"

"I didn't think of that," she admitted sheepishly.

"Great," I muttered, "and it's not like you can get the postcard back."

"Just tell her that he brought you here because he was being nice to me and Alex," Sam suggested. He was wearing the Statue of Liberty mask.

"I guess that makes sense," Twilight said.

"It would make more sense coming from somebody who wasn't wearing a Statue of Liberty mask," I commented.

Sam slipped off the mask.

"Can we get going now?" I asked.

"Are you feeling better, Alex?" Sam wondered.

I nodded.

"Good. Let's get going, then. I want to get to the top and look around." Twilight started off toward the Statue.

Sam hurriedly repacked the souvenirs in his shopping bag and we chased after Twilight. We caught up to her at the base of the Statue. She was standing there, staring up at its back. Two long lines of people were waiting to head up to the top. Above one line was a sign that read "Stairs to the Top," while the second line of people were taking the "Elevator to the Top."

"Shall we take the elevator?" Twilight asked.

"Funny," I answered. "Real funny. Let's get in line for the stairs."

Before Twilight could object, Sam started away to the stairs line. I joined him, and soon Twilight was standing in line beside us.

"I'll go along, but this is ridiculous. We should be taking the elevator. This is going to take a lot longer!" Twilight fumed. "Look at this line! Look at all the people ahead of us! There's thousands . . . thousands!"

I looked at the line. She was right. It snaked along between two fences, then rose up a slope and up some stairs before it disappeared into the base of the Statue.

"MR. CAVIN! MR. CAVIN!" Sam shouted. Sam was waving his arms in the air. What was he doing?

He turned to me. "It's Mr. Cavin, you know, from Wall Automotive. My parents get their cars fixed there. Maybe he'll let us in line with him."

Sam had opened his mouth to yell again when I grabbed him and spun him around.

"What are you doing?" I demanded. "If Mr. Cavin sees us, then he'll want to know where our parents are, and if you haven't noticed, we don't have any parents with us."

"Oh, yeah, I forgot."

"Sam, how far ahead is he?" I asked.

Sam pointed toward the top of the line. I looked between heads and saw Mr. Cavin with his wife and kids. One of them, Katie, went to our school. Mr. Cavin was standing at the partition, looking down at the line, scanning the crowd. Obviously he'd heard Sam call his name but couldn't figure out where the shout came from.

"Does he see us?" Twilight asked.

I shook my head. "I don't think so, but I'm positive he heard Sam yell his name. He's trying to figure out who it was."

"He'll know the minute one of you two leaves this line. There'll be no place to hide," Twilight observed.

"Then how can we get away?"

"Here," Sam said, handing me one of his souvenir masks. He smiled and slipped the second mask over his face. I slipped the other one on.

"See?" Twilight said. "I told you Sam got some neat stuff."

I hardly even minded the ferry ride back to the mainland. I was so relieved about getting away without being seen that I didn't even think about getting seasick until we were practically back to shore. What were the odds of running into somebody from Farmingdale in a city this big? Unbelievably bad luck, but we'd gotten away with it. My only regret was that Twilight still hadn't been to the top of the Statue. I wanted to get her to do at least one touristy thing in New York City.

We grabbed a hot dog from a sidewalk vendor and started to walk away from the ferry docks.

"Where shall we go to now?" Twilight asked.

"How about the apartment? I could use a nap before the concert," I suggested.

"A nap? What kind of granny are you? No way! How about the Empire State Building?" Twilight countered. "We could all *walk* to the top. I betcha we could make that in an hour . . . or two . . . or three . . . or four . . . or—"

"We get the idea. We're not going there, for sure," I said. It wasn't just that Sam wouldn't take the elevators—I didn't want to go up there either. I'd been up before. That time I made sure I stayed as far away as possible from the outside of the building. My father kidded me about how I should have checked out the view, enjoyed the sights. The only sight I liked was the sight of my feet back on the sidewalk.

"I have the perfect place. It's low to the ground, nobody has to take any elevators and it's probably the most amazing place in the whole world," Twilight gushed.

"Where?" I asked apprehensively.

"F. A. O. Schwarz."

"F. A. . . . . what?" Sam asked.

"F. A. O. Schwarz," Twilight answered.

"It's a toy store," I told Sam.

"It's not just *a* toy store. It's the greatest toy store in the universe!"

"I've heard of it," Sam said.

"I'd be shocked if you hadn't," Twilight said. "But you've never been there before?"

Sam shook his head.

"Me neither, but I heard it was pretty good," I said.

"Wait—your parents bring you to New York City but they've never taken you to F. A. O. Schwarz? I think I'm gonna cry. So, do you want to go?" she asked.

"Sounds okay to me," I reluctantly agreed. What I was really thinking was that it sounded safe to me. Even Twilight couldn't get us into any trouble in a toy store.

We stood in the square looking up at the big F. A. O. Schwarz sign. "So what's so special about this toy store?" Sam asked.

"Come on inside and I'll show you."

Twilight led us into a stream of people flowing in through the revolving doors. Just inside the store she stopped and we all looked around. It was an amazing sight! All around us were stuffed animals. We were standing in a virtual field of stuffed animals of all kinds and sizes. Off to one side, a life-sized merry-go-round spun. The ceilings soared high above our heads, and there were gleaming escalators and an elevator that looked like a gigantic robot.

"This looks familiar," Sam said.

"You've probably seen it before in movies or on TV," Twilight explained.

"Movies, that's right! I saw a movie where this kid gets changed into a man and he plays with the toys here!" I exclaimed.

"Yeah, I've seen them filming things in here all the time."

"Did you come here a lot?" I asked her.

"When I was little—before we moved to London—we used to come here every couple of weeks. My father let me buy almost anything I wanted. And whenever my mother sold a major piece of sculpture she'd bring me here as well. You wouldn't believe what this place looks like at Christmastime. It's something else."

"I'd like to see that," I added.

"Maybe we can take another trip before Christmas," Twilight suggested. "My father cancels these weekends all the time so his apartment is empty and—"

"NO!" I shouted.

People all around us stopped shopping and stared over at us.

"Let's just get through this one, okay?" I asked quietly.

Twilight laughed. "All right, Alex, darling. Anything you say."

"Where are the models and rockets?" Sam asked.

"I don't know, and I don't care," Twilight answered. "I'm here to look at the porcelain dolls."

"No way I'm going to waste my time looking at dolls!" I protested.

"Nobody's asking you to. I'll go to the dolls and you two go wherever you want. We'll meet up, in an hour, by the front doors. Okay?"

"Well . . . I don't know if we should separate."

"That's fine. If you think we should stay together, then I hope you and Sam enjoy the doll collection, because that's where I'm headed."

"Come on, Alex!" Sam protested. "We'll be safe. We're in a toy store!"

"He's right, Alex. What do you think is going to happen? Sam will be mauled by a teddy bear? You'll be shot by a toy soldier? I'll be run over by a remote-control car?"

"Okay, okay, okay. We'll split up and we'll meet you at the doors. It's one thirty-seven. We'll meet in exactly an hour. Let's synchronize our watches."

"This isn't a spy movie, Alex, it's a toy store. See you in an hour . . . or so!" Twilight smiled and disappeared into the crowd.

I looked at my watch. It was two forty-five! We were supposed to meet Twilight ten minutes earlier. After the models and remote-control cars and Lego-land and all the people demonstrating airplanes and special pens and new toys and everything, I'd lost track of the time. Keeping Twilight waiting was never a smart thing.

"We have to get going, Sam," I said.

"Wait . . . just let me see him do the trick one more time." He was fascinated, staring intently at a magician who was demonstrating various tricks. Sam was trying to figure out how they worked.

"We don't have time for this," I said, and dragged him through the crowd. We rode down on the escalator, past the gigantic stuffed animals, and came to the front doors.

"Do you see her?" I asked anxiously.

He shook his head. "Maybe she lost track of the time too."

"Maybe. Keep your eyes open."

"Look! Over there!" Sam exclaimed.

"Do you see her?"

"No, but look. There's a film crew!"

On a lower level, on the other side of the square, there was a big camera. It was in the middle of a roped-off area, surrounded by a large crowd.

"They must be making a movie! Let's go and see!"

"Sam! Come back!" I yelled. "We have to wait here for Twilight!"

Sam ignored my screaming. He sifted through the crowd without looking back. I had no choice but to go after him, but I caught up to him as he came to a stop at the back of the crowd.

"Sam, we have to wait by the doors."

"Can you see anything?" he asked, totally ignoring my statement.

"Nothing. Come on back. You can see more from where we were standing. All you can see here is people's backs."

A woman right in front of us turned around. "You kids want to get closer?"

"Yes!" Sam exclaimed.

She tapped the shoulder of the man in front of her. "Let 'em through, will ya? Let the kids get to the front!" The man turned sideways and asked the person in front of him to do the same.

"Let the kids through!" the woman hollered. "They want kids up front. Let 'em through!"

A small gap opened up all the way to the front. Before I even had a chance to argue, Sam started to squeeze through. I plunged in after him, trying unsuccessfully to grab his arm and stop him. Sam stopped at the rope barrier and I bumped into his back.

"Come on, Sam. We have to go back and meet Twilight," I pleaded.

"No . . . no . . . we can't."

"We have to!" I insisted.

"No, no, you don't understand," Sam said.

"I understand everything. Come on, we have to go back and meet Twilight."

"But, Alex, if we go back we'll miss her. She's *there*."

"There . . . where?" I swiveled my head around and then I saw her. Twilight was standing inside the rope circle. She was beside some woman holding a microphone, standing in front of the camera!

"TWILIGHT!" I screamed.

Every eye in the crowd turned to me.

"Cut!" a man yelled. He jumped up from beside the camera. The woman lowered the microphone.

"Come on, everybody, we need quiet!" the man said, looking out at the surrounding crowd. "Let's try it again."

"NO!" I shouted.

This time the man looked directly at me. "Please, son, we're on a deadline. We have to get these interviews on tape and back to station for the six o'clock news. Be good and we'll interview you next. Okay?"

"No! I don't want to be interviewed, and you can't interview her, either." I ducked under the rope and went to Twilight's side. "Come on, we have to go."

"Alex, please! I'm giving an interview. I'm going to be on television."

"Oh no you aren't!"

"We don't have time for this," the man said. He sounded angry. "Are we going to do this or not?"

"Yes!"

"No!" I yelled even louder.

"That's it! We don't have time! Get the next kid!" the man demanded.

"What? But . . . but . . . but . . ." Twilight stammered.

"Sorry, kid, we can't just wait while you argue with your boyfriend."

"He isn't my boyfriend!"

"Whatever. Just move along," the man said. He turned away from Twilight and started talking to his assistant.

Twilight opened her mouth to speak but didn't. Instead she turned to face me. There was an angry look in her eyes. I started to make my escape.

"Thanks a lot, Alex!" she snapped. "Do you know what you did?"

I didn't answer. I ducked back under the rope and tried to disappear into the crowd.

"You've spoiled my chance to be discovered!" she yelled.

I stopped and spun around. "That was the idea, Twilight. I was stopping you from being discovered by your mother, and my parents and Sam's parents."

"Get real, Alex. It was just a local cable news show. It only gets shown in New York and even here hardly anybody watches it. I'm not stupid. I checked before I agreed to give the interview."

"What were they interviewing you about?" Sam asked.

"It was about Christmas. They wanted to know what kids want for Christmas," Twilight answered.

"In that case I wish they'd interviewed me," I said.

"Why?"

"Because I *know* what I want for Christmas."

"What?" Sam asked.

"For all this to be just a bad memory."

Chapter Twelve

I held my breath as Twilight turned the key in the lock. She opened the door and we tentatively stepped into the apartment. I swiveled my head around anxiously, half expecting that crazed woman to come out of one of the rooms.

"She's not here, Alex. Relax."

"I'll relax," I answered. "Just wait until tomorrow night when I'm sleeping in my bed, in my room, in my house. Then I'll relax."

Twilight was still mad at me about the TV interview, and maybe I did overreact a bit, but I didn't think I was really wrong to stop her. On the other hand, I didn't want to spend the rest of the weekend dealing with her bad attitude about the whole thing.

"Twilight," I ventured, "I'm sorry about dragging you away from the TV crew."

"Well, you should be," she shot back. "That could have been a big break for me. Somebody could have seen that and wanted me for a part in a movie or something."

"You mean like a casting director?" I said.

"Yeah!"

"Like a casting director who might work in TV? Maybe on the soaps?"

She didn't answer this time.

"Maybe on your dad's soap? Somebody who might say, 'Hey, Brice, I saw your daughter—couldn't miss her with that hair and all the earrings—'"

"Okay," she said. "I get the point."

"All I mean is . . . sending postcards, showing up on TV . . . one way or another, it could get back to our parents, and we'd end up getting grounded till we're twenty-one."

"Yeah? Well, I've got a philosophy about that kind of thing," Twilight said, brightening up a bit.

"You do?" Sam asked.

"Yeah. I'll jump off that bridge when I get to it."

"Don't you mean you'll cross that bridge when you get to it?" I suggested.

"Alex, you live your life your way, I'll live my life my way!" Twilight told me. "Now, we'd better hurry. We don't have much time."

Sam looked at his watch. "We have plenty of time. The concert doesn't start for three more hours."

"Yeah, but we have to get ready. If we're going to a rock concert we have to look right."

"What do you mean?" I asked.

Instead of answering, Twilight walked out of the room and returned seconds later, carrying her backpack. "I thought we could start with your hair," she suggested.

"My hair! No way I'm going to wear any more wigs!" I protested.

Twilight walked right up and stopped in front of me. She placed a hand on my head and ruffled my hair.

"Alex. Darling Alex . . . I wouldn't ask you to cover up your lovely hair again."

I felt myself get all fuzzy and warm before the alarm bells in my head started to clang. Twilight took her hand from my head. She put her bag on the floor and bent down to look inside. She rummaged around and started to remove things: two long-handled combs, an extra-large tube of gel and a can of hair spray.

She looked up at me and smiled. "One more thing . . ." She reached her hand back into the bag. "Some hair dye."

"Hair dye!" I said in alarm.

"Don't worry, Alex," she said, handing me the box. "It's all washable. It'll come right out."

"I've heard that line before," I said, eyeing Sam and remembering my poor dog.

"No, really . . . read the box."

I looked at the back of the package. It did say it was washable. It contained five different colors of dye: blue, red, green, purple and orange.

"Before you say no, Alex, just give me a chance. I'll work on your hair for a while. If you really don't like it, you can wash it out before we go."

I handed her the package and walked out of the kitchen.

"Come on, don't be such a suck!"

I walked back into the room carrying a big red plastic milk crate I'd noticed in the corner by the empty boxes. I placed it on the floor in front of Twilight and sat down.

"I was just getting a seat. Go ahead," I announced.

What Twilight didn't know—what nobody except my barber knew—was that I loved to have my hair cut, combed, washed and brushed. Whenever I had my hair cut I'd just drift off into a fuzzy fog. I knew it would be even more wonderful with Twilight doing it.

She started combing my hair. I closed my eyes. I had to work hard not to make any weird sounds. I felt like a big old dog who was lying on the floor, his feet up in the air, having his tummy rubbed. Considering how badly I'd slept the night before, I wasn't surprised when I felt myself starting to drift off.

"Voilà!" Twilight announced, after what seemed like a dreamy twenty minutes or so.

I snapped out of my trance. "What does it look like?"

"WOW!" Sam exclaimed as he walked into the kitchen.

"I chased him out when I started . . . you didn't seem to notice," Twilight said. "I don't like to be watched when I'm working."

"What does it look like?" I repeated, reaching a hand up to my hair.

Twilight slapped my hand away. "Don't! You'll spoil it!"

"Wow! Me next!" Sam said.

"What does it look like?" I demanded for the third time, this time much louder. I rose to my feet.

"It's really hard to describe. Why don't you go and have a look?" Twilight suggested.

I sprinted out of the room and headed for the mirror in the bedroom. I stared at myself in shock. My hair was shaped into a series of tall spikes that formed a perfect row down the center of my head. The hair—both the spikes and the rest of it, which was plastered flat against my head—was bright, almost neon, blue. I looked like a sort of new-age dinosaur, like a stegosaurus on steroids. What I didn't look like was any kid from Farmingdale, New Jersey.

I noticed I had blue dye on the collar of my shirt, and even a few dribbles on my pants. How was I going to explain that to my parents? I'd have to hide the clothes and wash out the dye before putting them in the laundry hamper.

I grabbed my backpack and went into the bathroom. I locked the door and then double-checked it. I unbuttoned the shirt and took it off. Next I stripped out of my pants. Underneath I was wearing my Superman Underoos. Boy, I was glad it was Superman and not Twilight who had X-ray vision. I'd already taken enough kidding about my superhero clothing. I pulled on an old pair of jeans and grabbed my very favorite T-shirt, a black Harley-Davidson biker shirt with white letters on the back that read "BORN WILD." My parents hated this T-shirt almost as much as I liked it. Each time I put it on my mother said the same thing: "You weren't born wild, just a little early."

I started to pull the shirt on over my head but the added height of the spikes made it impossible for my head to fit through the hole. With my arms through the sleeves I opened the bathroom door and walked into the kitchen.

"This isn't working. My new head is too big for my old shirt," I announced.

Twilight looked up from her work on Sam to check out my problem. When she stepped aside I got my first glance at Sam's hair. It was spectacular. It had really taken shape—or I guess, really, color. Twilight had decided to use purple, red and green to create three broad sweeps of color. His head looked like the hairy flag of some emerging new country.

Twilight walked over to me. "Hmm . . . this shouldn't be too serious a problem. If your head is too big for the hole, we either have to make your head smaller, or . . . make the hole bigger."

There was a tearing sound as she ripped the neckband of my shirt. I gasped. Sam gasped. He knew how much I loved my shirt. Twilight pulled the shirt over my head, careful not to disturb the spikes.

"Nobody should go to a rock concert without at least one rip in their clothes. Now you have a rip," Twilight said, smiling broadly. She turned back to Sam.

I fingered the rip in my shirt. I wanted to say something, to yell at her, to let her know what she'd done. Instead I realized it was about time I *did* something wild instead of just wearing a T-shirt that *said* I was wild.

"There, that does it," Twilight said. Sam jumped up and rushed to find the mirror.

"WOW!" he screamed from the other room. He ran back into the kitchen. "I'd love to wear my hair like this to school."

"Or to church," I suggested.

Twilight started to work on herself. She couldn't be as careful with her own hair, so I think she decided to make up for it with extra everything. She plastered her hair down flat to her head with gel and then just splashed on color from the five tubes. We gave her a little bit of direction to fill in the gaps between the different patches. Where the colors overlapped, they blended together so they formed another ten new shades, different from the original five. It wasn't perfect or beautiful, but it certainly was original.

After changing clothes, and adding a few rips, Twilight and Sam were ready as well. Twilight was wearing a pair of black jeans, and the knees were so ripped that it was a miracle the bottoms of the legs were still hanging on. Her T-shirt looked like a giant Union Jack—probably one she got in London—and she topped it off with a short black leather jacket with so many buckles and zippers it would set off metal detectors a mile away. Sam insisted on wearing his new "I LOVE N.Y." T-shirt. I thought it was nice that Twilight didn't call him a tourist or give him a hard time about that.

I wanted to clean up the dye stains from the kitchen counter and floor but Twilight said we could do it later, if at all. She said her father wouldn't even notice, and if he did it would drive him crazy trying to figure out how they'd got there.

Leaving the apartment, Twilight locked the door. I jiggled the doorknob to check that it was locked, and we headed for the stairwell. We had ninety minutes to get to midtown, and into Madison Square Garden.

Chapter Thirteen

The traffic was jammed up as far as we could see—I'd never seen so many cars in one place at the same time. But even though we weren't moving much, the meter in our cab kept ticking away, running up the fare.

"Maybe we should get out and walk now," I suggested. "It isn't that much farther, is it?"

Twilight leaned over and tapped on the metal screen separating us from the driver. "How close are we?" she asked.

"Four, maybe five blocks. The kid's right—it probably would be faster to walk from here. I'll let you out."

Twilight started to unbuckle her backpack to get her wallet, but before she could I whipped out a ten-dollar bill. "Here." I pushed it through the slot. "And keep the change," I said, echoing what Twilight had said to the other cab driver. It made me feel like a bigshot.

"Thanks, kid."

We climbed out of the cab and took to the sidewalk. Already I could see some people who looked as if they were going to the same concert. More and more joined the crowd until, with Madison Square Garden in sight, there was almost nobody who didn't belong. Two stragglers, a middle-aged couple, looked worried as they gazed at the strange-looking creatures surrounding them, and hurried away.

The traffic along the street outside the Garden bumped along. Men with reflective orange jackets waved long-handled flashlights and tried to entice cars into various parking lots. Street vendors were everywhere, hawking T-shirts, programs, posters and buttons. Twilight stopped to browse at one of the stalls and we peeked over her shoulder. She bought a button with a picture of one of the bands on it. Every dozen or so paces we passed by some guy holding aloft a handful of tickets, yelling, "ANYBODY BUYING?" or something like that. This was obviously a hot show, and the scalpers were out in force.

At the front of the building the sidewalk became a solid mass of people moving toward the entrance. It was as if the Garden were a gigantic light and we were moths being pulled closer and closer. At the front doors we merged into one of the long lines shuffling inside. We first passed by ushers, who looked at our tickets. They tore them in half and handed the top part back to us. Next we joined a second set of lines. We had to pass between uniformed police officers. As we got closer I could see the officers were looking through every bag and parcel, and asking people to open or remove their coats. Some were even being patted down. Repeatedly the officers found bottles and cans, which they took and placed into two giant garbage cans. One of them was already overflowing with bottles.

We shuffled to the front of the line.

"Hi, kids. Aren't you three a little young to be here by yourselves?" one of the officers asked.

"We're not that young," Twilight countered.

"You look pretty young to *me*," the officer responded.

"We just look so young because you're so old," Twilight shot back.

The officer scowled. "Do your parents know where you are?"

"I hope so. They just went through the other checkpoint." Twilight pointed to the entrance farthest from where we stood.

"Yeah. We're meeting our parents at our seats," I added.

Twilight shot me a pleased but surprised look.

The one officer shook his head and looked at the

other. "I guess the family that listens to music together stays together."

"Let's have a look in your bags," one of the officers said.

I had a rush of fear. What would they think when they saw a change of clothing in our backpacks? We'd had to take them with us because we were afraid to leave them in the apartment in case that woman returned with a key and started snooping.

"You won't find any alcohol. It's just our clothes," Twilight said. "We came in for the weekend with my parents but we had to check out, so we had to take our clothes with us."

Boy, she was fast!

The officers rummaged through each of our bags and then handed them back. They weren't looking for clothes, or for kids who shouldn't be there by themselves. "Enjoy the concert," one of them said, and he waved us through.

As soon as we passed the checkpoint Sam took charge and launched into a guided tour of the Garden. He offered us the statistics, history, legends and stories of the structure. While all the others were making their way to their seats, we were walking from one end of the building to the other. Sam showed us a private box, the ice-making equipment in the basement, the dressing rooms and the outside of the executive offices.

During his tour, the warm-up band took the stage, and more people settled into their seats. I could tell Twilight was getting more and more impatient and she wanted to get to our seats, too.

"Come on, Alex, try to keep up. I've got one more place to show you. Even *you* haven't been there before. You'll love it!" Sam said as he pushed through a door and disappeared.

"Come on, Alex, you'll *love* it," Twilight echoed in mocking tones as she followed after Sam.

I'd had enough. I opened the door and saw that they were now in a long corridor, with another door at the end. "Hold on, Sam. We're missing the concert!" I protested.

Behind me, I heard the door we'd just come through open once again.

"Hello, little Sammy. How are you and your annoying friends?" came a voice from over my shoulder.

I felt a chill travel up my spine and into the back of my head, where it numbed my brain. I knew, even without looking, that it was Skully standing right behind me. Sam and Twilight turned, and I could see the fear in their eyes. Slowly I twisted around. He stood there, big and ugly and angry and glaring. I felt a rush of fear sweep through my entire body. At least he didn't have the rest of his gang with him.

"Ain't you gonna say hello? You three ain't got no

manners at all. Twice I met ya and twice ya treat me bad. I'm just goin' to have to *teach* you all some manners." His voice was gravelly, and the words were being forced out through clenched teeth.

"First off, ain't *you* gonna say hello to me!" Skully snarled. He reached out and grabbed me by the arm and pulled me, hard, toward him. I stumbled and I felt myself falling forward fast, and then there was a shooting pain in the top of my head and a sickening thud as my thick skull crashed into the delicate flesh and cartilage of Skully's face! My teeth jarred together and I bit the edge of my tongue. There was an explosion of blood, and Skully, like a sack of potatoes, collapsed into my arms and then crumpled into a puddle on the gray concrete floor. I stepped back in fear and shock and peered down at him. There was total silence. Even the dull thuds from the first band had stopped. A low moan from Skully filled the silence.

"I . . . I wasn't trying to hurt him," I stuttered as I wiped some of the blood off my hands and onto my shirt. "It was an accident . . . I stumbled . . . it was an accident."

"Wow!" Sam exclaimed.

"But he was trying to hurt you. It was self-defense!" Twilight cried.

"I better call somebody . . . we better get him some help," I said nervously.

"You're the one that's going to need help," Skully mumbled from the floor. He lifted himself onto one elbow. Blood was pouring from his nose and mouth.

I leaped backward, almost knocking Twilight over. Skully pulled himself up to his feet and staggered unsteadily. I braced myself for Skully to advance, but instead he stumbled back the few steps to the door to the concourse. He pushed it open. Instantly it was filled with the shapes of his gang. Skully slumped against the wall, sliding down to the floor.

"Alex! Twilight! Run!" Sam screamed. I turned around. He was at the far end of the corridor, holding the next door open.

Twilight and I broke toward Sam just as the gang members broke toward us. The sounds of our feet hitting the floor echoed through the corridor. Then I heard the sound of bodies falling and cursing and I glanced over my shoulder. Behind me, at the door, was a mass of intertwined arms, legs and bodies. They had tripped over Skully as they'd scrambled through the narrow doorway. They worked to get themselves free as we sped through the next doorway and Sam slammed the door shut behind us. There was a loud crash as they collided with the door, and the handle shook violently.

I scanned the room desperately for a way to escape. Sam took a seat and put his feet up on a counter. What was he doing?

"We have to get out!" I yelled. "How can we get away?"

"Take a seat, relax," he invited as he patted the seat beside him. "We're safe. They can't get in through that door. It's locked."

I let out a sigh of relief.

"But if it's locked, how did we get in?" Twilight asked.

"It's a combination lock and I knew the combination," he explained. "All the secure doors in the whole building have the same code: 6, 9, 4. That's the last time the Rangers won the Stanley Cup, in the sixth month of 1994."

"But how did *you* know that was the combination?" Twilight asked.

"My father told me. His bank provided the financing for the renovations. He brought me here on a tour once, and I remembered."

"You sure they can't get in after us?" Skully's friends were pounding on the door, and I could still make out voices—muffled yells—coming from the other side.

"Not unless *they* know the combination," Sam said.

"No danger there," Twilight added. "I doubt any of them even know how to count."

I sat down to catch my breath. I was panting, not so much from running as from fear. I wanted my heart to stop beating so fast, to settle down.

I looked around. We were in some sort of TV booth. There were banks of televisions and a big panel with lots of dials and swivel chairs parked in front of the controls. The whole front of the room was a large Plexiglas partition.

"Welcome to Rangers hockey," Sam said.

"What?"

"Rangers hockey . . . also Knicks basketball. This is the broadcast booth for the games."

Twilight walked over and looked through the windows wrapped around the booth. She motioned for me to come over. We had an incredible view of the Garden. The stage was directly below us. In the dim light, the crowd below looked like rolling waves. Up at our level, right under the rafters, was a haze of smoke that had risen up from the crowd. It was a good thing we were sealed in away from all that smoke. All I needed was to have an asthma attack.

I could clearly see the concert going on beneath us, but I couldn't hear a thing. I knew one of the bands was playing, though, because I could feel the thump of the bass coming through the floor.

"Sam, how come it's so quiet in here?" I asked.

"It's specially soundproofed to keep out the crowd noises during the games."

"Just our luck," Twilight noted with disappointment. "Here we are, stuck in this booth and we can't even hear the concert."

"Just push open the partition if you want to hear," Sam suggested.

"What?" Twilight asked.

"The partition, the Plexiglas, right beside you. Release the handle and it slides open."

Twilight fumbled around with the handle and the whole panel, just like a patio door, slid off to one side. The music and smoke and haze and crowd noise all swelled in through the opening. Twilight leaned forward, out the partition and into open space. I shuddered, and I saw Sam lean back, away from the opening, as if he were in danger of falling across the whole width of the booth and then out the window.

"Hey, Sam, what's that?" Twilight asked, gesturing with her hand out the opening.

Sam got to his feet but didn't move any closer. "That's the catwalk. It runs all through the rafters, like an elevated sidewalk."

I moved over beside Twilight and looked at the catwalk. It was narrow, just wide enough for one person, lined by two waist-high guardrails. The metal floor seemed solid enough, but as I looked more closely I noticed it was some sort of grating. I allowed my eyes to follow the catwalk up and away from where we stood and into the rafters. I narrowed my eyes and tried to keep following the path where it traveled—through the rafters and the smoky haze—over toward the far side of the building.

"Sam, where does this lead to?" I asked.

"I don't know," Sam said quietly.

I spun around to face him. He was staring down at his feet.

"Sam . . . *you* don't know where it leads?"

Still looking down, Sam spoke quietly. "Sorry, Alex. It's just . . . if I tell, you'll want to go."

"Go where?"

"It leads to a way out . . . lots of ways out."

"Out?" Twilight said. "Out? Let's go!" she shouted excitedly as she bounded the first few steps up the catwalk.

"Wait!" I shouted.

Surprisingly, Twilight froze in place. I moved back to Sam's side. I put my hand on his shoulder.

"Sam, you know we can't stay here, and we can't go back the way we came."

He nodded his head.

"I know you're scared of heights. I don't like them either. Maybe we can help each other out. Okay?"

Again, Sam nodded in agreement. He started for the opening. Then he stopped and propped his hands against the window frame. I looked over his shoulder. Twilight was sitting on the catwalk, hanging onto the railing, her feet dangling over the edge, into space.

"Okay, boys, let's get a-movin'," Twilight said. She got back to her feet and started walking.

The ramp rose at a gentle incline up to the center of the building. Twilight raced ahead, stopping periodically to peer over the side at the ongoing concert. I moved slowly, Sam right behind me. I moved foot by foot, my hands on the railings. Suspended as it was, the catwalk had a certain amount of sway and give. With each step it sank and then rose ever so slightly. I couldn't hear anything except the pounding beat of the music, but I felt Twilight's footfalls reverberating throughout the length of the walkway, and each one created a vibration that moved up my leg and settled into the pit of my stomach. I tried not to think about falling, but I kept having a vision of myself cartwheeling end over end through the air as I fell through space, accelerating at 5.2 feet per second, the ground rushing up to meet me. I thought about the people down below who would break my fall and about how the crowd would react. I wondered if they'd stop the concert or just sweep me up with the popcorn and candy wrappers at the end of the show. I drove the thought out of my mind again and concentrated on putting one foot in front of the other.

"Are you doing okay, Sam?" I yelled back to him.

He was standing as still as a statue, his hands on the railings, staring down through the flooring. I crossed back until I stood in front of him.

"Come on, Sam, just come with me."

I reached over and took one of his hands. Like a little toy balloon he trailed behind me. Soon the incline flattened out. Now, with each step the smoke and haze were getting thicker. Here, at the very center of the building, the highest point of the catwalk, at the halfway mark, it was so thick I could hardly see a dozen yards ahead of me. Surprisingly, it didn't seem to be bothering my throat or sinuses or lungs.

"What is this stuff?" I yelled to Sam.

"What?" He was having trouble hearing me over the music.

"This smoke. What is it?" I yelled louder.

"Mostly dry ice," he yelled back. "It's almost like the steam from a humidifier!"

That explained why it wasn't bothering me. "Do you want to stop and have a rest?" I screamed into his ear.

"No, don't stop, just keep on walking. If I stop I might not start again."

We continued on. The catwalk started to slope downward. Looking ahead, I could make out Twilight's outline, almost obscured by the beams and the haze, already at the far side, waiting. I decided to focus on her . . . just look at her . . . and think about how when I got to Twilight my feet would almost be back on solid concrete.

Twilight looked back at us and gave a little wave. She then motioned for us to hurry up and join her. I was moving as fast as I could. Then, as I continued to watch, Twilight did the unthinkable—she reached a leg over the railing and hauled herself up until she was sitting on the railing of the catwalk! My stomach did a flip just watching her perched there. Then she wavered, swung an arm backward, to try to regain her balance and fell over the edge!

Chapter Fourteen

I felt my stomach rush up into my throat. I froze in place, rooted to the catwalk, until Sam bumped into me. He hadn't seen her fall because I was blocking his view. Jolted into action, I raced across the catwalk to reach the spot where Twilight had fallen. I grabbed the railing with both hands and braced myself. I didn't want to look but I knew I had to. I forced myself to peer over the railing.

"Hi, Alex!" Twilight was sitting on a low, wide ledge just a few feet below the catwalk. "When I saw you staring at me I thought I'd give you a little rush. Did I freak you out?"

I was speechless. I'd thought she was dead, and it was

only some stupid trick. I was glad—no, make that thrilled—she was alive, but now I wanted to kill her myself. I could tell by the look in Twilight's eyes that she knew I wasn't amused by any of this. At all.

Sam had managed to cover the distance and now stood beside me. Although he hadn't seen Twilight's fall, he had seen me run as if my pants were on fire, and I was sure he'd been scared.

"Alex, what happened?"

Twilight spoke before I could answer. "I already checked and there's a door out to the concourse. Nobody's waiting for us. It's safe."

"Thanks for being so considerate, Twilight," I answered. "You're always so *considerate*."

"What are you doing down there, Twilight?" Sam asked.

"Just playing a joke on Alex."

"Some joke. Really funny. Downright hilarious . . . I thought you were dead."

"I'm not, so be happy. Smile. Come on, Alex, give me one of your wonderful little smiles," she coaxed me. She flashed a brilliant grin at me.

I scowled, but as I looked at Twilight, her smile growing even wider, I felt myself begin to smile too. It was completely out of my control.

"Now isn't that better?" Twilight said.

And as I smiled at her, I thought, *Yes! Twilight isn't*

dead; we're alone in New York for the weekend; I'm standing here with blue spiked hair, on a catwalk 120 feet above a sold-out rock concert and I just beat up the leader of a street gang! I started to laugh, first low and soft, and then louder and louder. I lifted a leg over the guardrail of the catwalk, pulled myself over and then hopped down to the ledge. I started to laugh even louder and tears started to roll out of the corners of my eyes. Still I couldn't stop laughing.

Twilight looked worried. I knew she had to be thinking I was cracking up.

"Alex, are you okay?" Sam asked from the catwalk.

I looked up at him with his tricolored hair and started laughing even harder. Both he and Twilight stared at me with increasing concern until I finally got a grip.

"Alex, are you all right?" Twilight asked.

"All right? All right! Think about what we've done this weekend! Think about what we're doing this very moment! Think about what we still have to do!" I shook my head slowly. "It's all pretty amazing, and do you know what's most amazing?"

"What?" Sam asked.

"For the first time since we even started talking about this weekend, I actually believe we're going to get away with it. If we haven't got caught or killed up to now, I don't think anything can stop us."

"That's the attitude, Alex," Twilight said, patting me on the back. "That's exactly, completely, one hundred percent the right attitude. Come on, let's get going." She reached a hand up to grab the railing.

"No . . . not just yet. I came here to see a concert and I think we should stay here until it's over," I told her.

"Fantastic idea!" Twilight beamed.

"But shouldn't we be trying to get away before Skully can find us again?" Sam asked.

"He can't find us here. Besides, once the concert ends there'll be a bigger crowd for us to get lost in," I answered.

We all sat down, Twilight and I on the ledge and Sam on the catwalk above us, to enjoy the rest of the concert.

The concert had gone on for three hours—including two lengthy encores. Then, after smashing their instruments into little tiny pieces, the last band left the stage for good.

The speakers fell silent and the only sounds were the buzz of the crowd and the ringing in my ears. The house lights came on. The people down below filtered out toward the exits.

"Okay, now we go," I said.

We climbed up to the catwalk and went through a door to the concourse. We quickly found an escalator and started down to the ground floor.

Looking around only confirmed what I'd already

known. We were the youngest, and smallest, people in the crush of bodies. Our heads were well below the surface of the crowd and we were swallowed up by the throng of concertgoers.

"Let's stick close. There's no telling where Skully or his gang might be," I said. "Sam, you know the best way out, so we'll follow you. I still can't believe that in a city this big we had the bad luck to run into those guys again."

"Not really bad luck," Sam said sheepishly. "I think I sort of mentioned to them that we were going to the concert."

"Maybe you should have sort of mentioned to us that you said that."

"Sorry."

We weaved in and out of the crowd and made our way to a side exit. We popped out the door. The cool night air felt wonderfully refreshing. The Garden, heated up by sixteen thousand fans, was like a steam bath, especially up in the rafters where we'd been sitting.

"All right, we made it!" Twilight crowed.

Before either of us could answer, we heard somebody yell: "Hey, Sammy! Stay right there!"

All three of us turned. I was filled with horror. Two huge men were barreling through the crowd toward us. They had beards and black T-shirts and jeans. They looked terrifying! They were so tall that their heads were above the crowd as much as ours were below it. People just got out of their way as they waded through, afraid that they'd be crushed.

"You three, stay right where you are!" bellowed the bigger of the two, pointing a meaty finger right at us.

I couldn't believe this. These guys had to work for Skully. We were dead, or worse than dead. They were only a few feet away when my mind clicked back to life. It was like one of those nature documentaries where a trapped animal has to choose between fight or flight. Fighting wouldn't work.

"Run!" I screamed. We turned as one and ran.

"Freeze!" I heard one of them yell from over my shoulder.

We dodged and weaved though the crowd. Being so much smaller than everybody else, we were partially hidden as we ran. I could hear them behind us, like two grizzly bears crashing through a forest, pushing and shoving people out of their way. We turned around a corner and I ducked behind a parked car. Twilight followed suit instantly. I grabbed Sam by the arm and pulled him down just before the men rounded the corner. They plowed straight ahead, through the crowd, right past our hiding place. Immediately we got up and doubled back the way we'd just come.

"Stop right there!" an angry voice shouted.

Three more men, as large as the other two, were now moving toward us. This couldn't be happening. It was like a bad dream . . . like a nightmare!

"There they are! Over there!" The original two thugs were coming back at us, and they'd brought along three others. Large, menacing men were closing in on us from all sides.

"Quick, Alex, give me your wallet," Twilight demanded.

"My wallet? We can't buy our way out of this!"

"Don't argue. Just give me your wallet!" she implored.

I fumbled in my pocket, pulled it out and handed it to Twilight. The ring of muscular men closed in around us. Twilight ripped the money out of my wallet and waved it above her head.

"MONEY, FREE MONEY, COME AND GET IT, FREE MONEY!" she yelled at the top of her lungs. And before I could think or say anything she'd tossed the money into the air. The breeze caught hold of the bills, which swirled and danced before floating down to settle to the ground.

The effect was electric. Everything and everybody seemed to freeze. Then they all came unstuck at once and the crowd surged toward us. Hundreds of people chased after the bills, pushing, shoving, screaming and yelling.

"Stay low and stick with me!" Twilight commanded as she dropped to her hands and knees.

"Are you crazy?"

She pulled me down to the ground and we started to crawl. All around us were feet and legs, scrambling and shoving. We were going to be crushed!

"Ouch!" I screamed as somebody stepped on my hand.

Twilight turned around. "Just keep moving!" she ordered.

I looked back at Sam, who was on his hands and knees as well. Two bodies went tumbling over top of him and crashed to the ground. Sam crawled toward me at full speed and we all scurried away, keeping low, finding little openings between the people, or between the legs of those who were grabbing at the few dollars lingering in the air or littering the ground. Just as I thought I'd be smothered or crushed I popped past the last person and came out into an open space. I started to get up.

"Stay low!" Twilight hissed.

Sam crawled right up and bumped into me. I turned back around. In the middle of the mob stood those big men, pushing and shoving along with the rest of the crowd. I scrambled after Sam and Twilight as they crawled on all fours into a parking lot. Cars were jockeying, trying to get out, creating a traffic jam in the lot and onto the street. From the parking lot we exited down a back alley and away from the crowd.

"Did we make it?" Sam asked breathlessly.

"Not yet, but getting closer. The faster we're back in the apartment the happier I'll be," I answered.

"Do we go to the subway?" asked Sam.

"Too risky. They might be looking for us there," Twilight said. "How about we walk for a few blocks and then hail a cab?"

"Sounds good to me," Sam replied, and we started to run down the alley.

I couldn't believe how much energy and endurance fear can give you. I felt as though I could fly. Six or seven blocks from the Garden we stopped running and tried to get a cab. That wasn't so easy. It seemed that nobody wanted to pick up three kids in the middle of the night, and empty cabs kept refusing to stop for us. Finally we got one and he drove us the last fifteen blocks. We had him drop us off a block away from the apartment and we walked.

I glanced at my watch as we entered the lobby of the building. It was almost two in the morning. The lobby was deserted and our footfalls echoed off the walls. Twilight headed for the elevator and pushed the button. Sam stood stock-still in the middle of the lobby.

"Come on, guys. It's late, we're all tired and the sooner we get behind the locked apartment door the better off we'll be," Twilight reasoned.

I had to admit she made sense. I wanted to ride up too.

"What do you think, Sam? After the catwalk this should be easy," I said.

Sam stopped and looked at me. He looked like a tired little puppy who'd been left out in the rain.

"I'll meet you two up there," he said, and he moved toward the stairs.

I watched Sam walk away. I heard the *ping* of the elevator and turned to see Twilight standing there, holding the door open. I was tired. My head was sore where I'd head-butted Skully. My backpack weighed a ton. All I wanted to do was to go to sleep, but I knew what I had to do.

"See you up there," I called out. I ran up to Sam and caught him as he pushed through the door. Before the door had even closed behind us, Twilight caught up.

"Friends have to stick together," she said as she fell in beside us.

My legs felt heavy and the staircase seemed longer and with higher steps than it had the first time up. We moved slowly, each of us going at his own pace. When I finally reached the eighteenth floor I looked at my watch: it was 2:18. Twilight and Sam were somewhere below me and Twilight had the key. All I wanted was to lie down and go to sleep. I leaned against the door and slid down to the floor.

Then I heard voices. At first I thought it was just those of my friends bouncing up the stairwell, but the voices faded when I pulled away from the door. I turned and pressed my ear against it. There was no mistake. They were definitely coming from the hall, from the eighteenth-floor hallway. I pulled the door partway open and the voices became louder, although I couldn't make out any words. I closed the door without making a sound. Slowly and silently I retreated down the stairs. I ran into Twilight and Sam, three floors below.

"There's somebody up on the eighteenth floor. I heard them," I said anxiously.

"Gee, big news. There's lots of people on the eighteenth floor. There must be fifteen apartments on that floor," Twilight said as she moved past me, continuing to climb.

"But what about the time!? What are people doing in the hall at this time of night?"

"Alex," Twilight began, using the tone of voice one would usually reserve for a small child, "try to remember that this is New York and not Farmingdale. This is the city that never sleeps. They don't roll up the sidewalks at nine o'clock here."

Twilight kept on climbing and made the turn to the next landing. Sam continued to trudge along as well.

"Come on, Alex, Twilight knows what she's saying. We have to get to bed. The bus leaves early tomorrow morning."

I wasn't prepared to give up. I pushed past Sam and bounded up the steps, two at a time, until I overtook Twilight.

"Look, we can't just walk out there. It could be them

. . . Skully, or even worse, those monster men. They could be waiting for us," I said, panting to catch my breath. I knew I didn't sound very convincing, only scared.

"Alex, get a grip," Twilight replied.

"She's right, Alex. There's no way they'd know where we're staying," Sam said.

"Maybe they followed us," I argued.

"Alex, I want you to take a deep breath, maybe even take a little squirt from that puffer thing of yours, and then think about this a little bit. If they followed us, wouldn't it make just a little more sense for them to be *behind* us right now instead of in *front* of us, waiting? These guys looked *psycho*, not *psychic*." Twilight sighed.

They both continued to walk. I knew what I was saying and feeling didn't make sense, but then, what sense did it make in the first place to come on this weekend? I sprinted up the stairs and stopped them once again, just one flight short of our destination.

"Nobody goes on that floor before we check," I said with an air of quiet determination.

"Alex . . ." Twilight started to answer, in that patronizing tone she had.

"No! So far I have gone along with every crazy thing you two have wanted. Now I want you to humor me, even if what I'm saying doesn't make any sense! Nobody goes onto that floor until I make sure it's safe!"

Both of them looked shocked but nodded in agreement.

"For all we know it could even be that woman, waiting for us," I said.

Twilight's eyes widened. "I guess it could be."

"Come on, let's be quiet and listen at the door."

I led the way and we silently moved up the last few steps. I pulled open the door ever so slightly. The voices were gone. Through the crack in the door I saw partway down the hall, just to the other side of the elevators. I dropped to my knees and then lay flat against the concrete floor. The cold from the floor crept through my clothes. I thought of that warm, soft bed waiting for me, urging me to simply get up and walk to the apartment. I didn't hear anything and I didn't see anything. That was what bothered me—what I couldn't see. I couldn't see the far end of the hall where Brice's apartment was located. The only way I could see it would be to step out into the hall. But then anybody who was there would see me as well.

"Okay?" Twilight whispered.

"Not yet," I whispered back. I let the door close silently. "I want you to wait a couple of minutes and then open the door just a little so you can see the elevators, but not enough that anybody can see you. Okay?"

"But why?" Twilight asked.

"Just do it. I'm going to make sure it's safe," I whispered.

I shot down the stairs before any more questions could be asked. I raced down three flights. Renewed fear had given me renewed energy. With only a quick check I went into the hallway on the fifteenth floor and pressed the button for the elevators. The lights above the doors showed all three elevators were waiting in the lobby. One of them started up in answer to my call.

"Come on, hurry up," I said to myself as I anxiously waited for it to reach me. The floor-number lights lit up as it climbed toward my floor. I felt a rush of fear as the door opened—it was okay, it was empty. I jumped in and pushed the buttons for floors sixteen, seventeen and eighteen and then jumped from the elevator as the door started to close.

I ran up the stairs as quickly and as quietly as I could. When I got to the landing, Twilight was peeking through the barely opened door and Sam was standing beside her. I got there just in time to hear a voice. A shiver went up my spine.

"Okay, everybody get into position—one of the elevators is moving," somebody in the hall said.

Suddenly five burly men were standing in front of the elevator doors. It was the guys from outside the Garden! They stared up at the floor-number lights.

"They're stopping at every floor," said one of them angrily.

"Has to be those kids. Who else but kids would fool around at two in the morning?" a second one added.

The elevator arrived with a *ping* and two of them bounded onto it.

"It's empty!" thundered a voice.

Twilight let go of the door and it closed noiselessly. We headed back down the stairs.

"What now?" Twilight asked.

"I'm not sure, but I do know we have to leave this building and find someplace else to sleep," I said.

"Where?" Sam asked.

"I don't know, but someplace away from here."

It wasn't long before Sam was softly snoring, right beside me, his head against my shoulder. I wasn't sure but I thought Twilight was asleep as well. I was far too uneasy to close my eyes. I stared out the window, trying to see if anything, or anybody, was coming at us, out of the darkness. It wasn't home. It wasn't even Brice's apartment. It was a Volvo sedan, the first car we'd passed with its doors unlocked.

Chapter Fifteen

I opened my eyes and shielded them from the bright morning light. The sun peeked out from over the top of a building. The Volvo certainly had lots of head and leg room but not as much sleeping room as I would have liked. Or heat—sleeping in a car through the night in October was not my idea of cozy. I opened the back door and stepped out. I arched my back and worked my legs up and down to shake out the kinks. That seemed to wake up the other two. Twilight got out of the front seat while Sam crawled across the back seat and hung his legs out the door.

"I'm hungry," Sam announced.

"Me too. Let's find someplace to get breakfast," Twilight suggested.

In the bright light of the morning sun I caught a good look at my two friends. They'd looked ridiculous enough yesterday, but now, after a night sleeping in a car, they were even more freakish. The dye had leaked out of their hair and onto their faces. I bent over and looked at myself in the side-view mirror. My eyes widened in shock. I was just as freaky-looking as they were!

"I think we have to catch a shower before we get breakfast. We can't arrive home looking like this," I said.

Sam looked at his watch. "It's six-thirty. We have to eat, change, clean up and get to the station before the bus leaves at a quarter to nine. We'd better get moving."

"The terminal has restrooms," Twilight said. "We can wash our hair and change there."

"And eat," Sam added. "I saw a restaurant there called Kramden's Kafe."

Sam climbed out of the Volvo and slammed the back door. Twilight closed the front door as well. We'd only gone a few paces when I spun around and ran back to the car. I walked completely around it and checked all the doors. One opened. I clicked down the lock and closed it again. Then I saw the smile on Twilight's face.

"Just shut up!" I muttered.

"I didn't say a thing," she said, holding her hands up.

"Yeah, but I know what you're thinking."

The sidewalks along Greenwich Avenue were deserted. The only movement on the street was from an occasional car whizzing by. Maybe New York is a city that never really sleeps, but that morning it had at least one eye closed.

We covered nine blocks before Greenwich hit Eighth Avenue. Up ahead I saw the Fourteenth Street subway entrance. We headed down. A smile came to my face as we pushed through the turnstiles. Only two days ago I was terrified to be on the subway, and now I felt a sense of relief.

We'd hardly reached the platform when a local train pulled into the station. We boarded a near-empty car and rode the three stops to Forty-second Street and the Port Authority Bus Terminal.

The terminal building was as empty as the streets. We headed immediately for the restrooms. The women's and men's were across a narrow corridor from each other. We split up. Twilight hesitated as she pushed against the door and looked back at us.

I knew what she was thinking. "Don't worry," I said. "Skully and his type wouldn't be up this early. And if I were you I'd be more worried about frightening someone yourself. You look terrible!"

Twilight's expression changed from nervous to annoyed. "Yeah, right, look who's talking," she said, her eyes flaming. She turned and went into the restroom.

I smiled and pushed through the door. Sam was already standing in front of the mirror that ran the length of the room. We both stripped off our torn T-shirts. Mine was streaked with Skully's blood. I balled it up and tossed it toward a garbage can sitting at the far end of the counter. It hit the side and slumped to the floor. My parents would be happy never to see that shirt again. Sam took his and threw it at the can too. It hit the rim and its momentum rolled it over the top and into the can.

"And the crowd goes wild!" I said.

"Crowd . . . what crowd."

"You know, in sports when somebody . . . just forget it."

I turned on the taps. Nothing came out of the hot-water tap, so I filled the sink with cold water. Using the hand soap from the dispensers I started to "shampoo" my hair. Sam did the same. The thick pink soap felt greasy in my hands, but it lathered up pretty well. The water in the sinks became colored with the dye washing out of our hair. Purply red water slopped onto the counter and down onto the floor.

Working quickly, I tried to get the soap out of my hair with the cold water, then dried myself with the paper towels from the dispenser.

"What are you boys doing?"

I jumped. A man was standing by the door. His arms were folded across his chest and he looked angry. Very angry. He wore a red cap and a white shirt with a name tag pinned to the chest.

"I said, what are you boys doing?" His voice was even louder and angrier now.

"We're just . . . just . . . washing up," I sputtered, as I tried to cover myself with the damp paper towels I was holding.

"Washing up? What you two are doing is making a mess in my restroom. Who do you think is going to clean up all this mess?"

"I . . . I guess we are."

"You're darn right! The two of you are going to clean it. Just 'cause I'm the attendant doesn't mean I have to clean up after everybody. Your parents don't work here, so you have to clean up after yourselves. You understand?"

Sam and I both nodded vigorously.

"Good! The two of you pull on your shirts. I'll go and get you a bucket and a couple of mops. Understand?"

Again we agreed. Once he'd left the room, Sam and I exchanged looks and then pulled out clean shirts from our backpacks. In a minute the attendant reappeared, pushing a bucket containing two mops. Sam hurried over and held the door open so he could get in more easily, then grabbed a mop and started on the floor.

"You waiting for an invitation?" the man asked me.

"No, sir," I replied. I grabbed the other mop.

The man leaned against the counter and watched us work. "You kids sleep here last night?"

I paused. "In the restroom?"

"No, in the bus station."

"No, sir," I replied.

"Hummppphhh . . . kinda polite for runaways."

"We're not runaways!" Sam objected.

"Whatever you say, kid. It don't matter to me what you are as long as you don't make a mess in my restroom."

"But, honestly, we aren't runaways. We're on our way home! We're just washing up while we wait for our bus," I explained.

"Bus to where?"

"Farmingdale. We're going to catch the eight forty-five to Farmingdale, New Jersey," Sam answered.

"Good . . . that gives you lots of time to finish here."

He stood over us and supervised while we mopped away. After watching for a while he grabbed a rag and helped clean off the counter. He asked us questions and made small talk. He seemed like a nice man—I figured he was worried about us. Finally Sam pulled out his ticket and showed him that we really were going to catch a bus. We finished and left the bathroom.

Twilight was already waiting. She was sitting on the floor, with her back against the wall. She was in clean clothes, but still had multicolored hair.

"What took you so long?" she asked. "I was beginning to think you'd gone down the drain!"

"It's a long story," I said. "I'll save it for the bus ride."

"Twilight," Sam said, "you're still all rainbow! You didn't wash your hair!"

She smiled. "My mother would be suspicious if I didn't come home with my hair different," she smiled. "Let's go and eat."

We didn't need to think twice. We walked across the bus station to the restaurant, Kramden's Kafe. It was bright and clean. We took a seat in a booth in the corner, overlooking the main floor of the terminal. As we settled in, the waitress gave us three menus shaped like buses. The special was the Busman's Breakfast: three eggs done any way, ham or bacon, hash browns, toast, juice and a bottomless cup of coffee. I thought it was a good idea to give bus drivers all the coffee they wanted. That way, they might have to stop to go to the bathroom a lot, but they wouldn't fall asleep.

"Order anything you want," Twilight suggested. "I'm paying."

"Good," I remarked, "'cause *somebody* threw all my money away."

We ordered three of the specials. My stomach was grumbling like mad. I was very grateful when the food arrived, and even more grateful that it was delicious. We all turned our attention to eating. After we'd scraped the last bits of food from our plates, we continued to sit in our booth, and watched the lobby below as it started to come to life. The ticket agents opened for business. The first buses of the day arrived and their passengers passed through the terminal doors. People purchased tickets and sat or paced, waiting for their buses.

Sam looked at his watch. "It's time to get going."

Twilight put down money to cover the bill, and we all got up to leave. We strolled out into the lobby and through the doors to the bus bay. Although there were two buses in the bays with their engines running, the air still smelled fresh. I could see a bus waiting at platform 240, where we'd be leaving. We were only a few feet from safety.

"Hey! Wait a second!" came a voice behind us.

We all turned around. Standing right there was a policeman. He walked over to us. "Do you three need any assistance?"

"Ah . . . no, thank you. We're just fine. We're getting on our bus right now," Twilight said.

"Bus? Where are you headed to?" he asked.

"Farmingdale, Officer, sir," I answered.

"Farmingdale. I know Farmingdale. Pretty little place."

"Yes, sir. We're going home, sir," I said nervously.

"And what exactly were you doing here in New York? Who was looking after you?" he asked.

"My grandparents. They just dropped us off. We were visiting them and they showed us around the city," Twilight answered.

The officer nodded slightly and then bent over until he was low enough to look right into Sam's face. "You've been pretty quiet. What's your name, son?"

"Sam."

"And your friends?"

"Alex and Twilight."

"Sam, Alex and Twilight," he repeated. A smile came to his face. "Well, Sam, Alex and Twilight, I'm going to walk the three of you to your bus and make sure you get on it safe and sound. Come!" he ordered.

Obediently, we trailed behind him. We got to the door of the bus and the officer motioned for us to enter. The driver was already at his seat, sipping a cup of coffee and reading a section of the Sunday New York Times. The officer stepped up onto the bus right behind us.

"Good morning. Is this bus bound for Farmingdale?" the officer asked.

The driver put down his paper and looked at him. "Yep, Farmingdale is one of my stops, but shouldn't you be taking a police car instead of a bus?" he joked.

"Funny, very funny. I have three special passengers," he said, and he turned to us. "Give the nice man your tickets."

Twilight and Sam handed him theirs and started for the back of the bus. I put down my backpack. My ticket was safely in the bottom of my bag and I had to shuffle things around to get to it.

"How many stops before Farmingdale?" the officer asked.

"Lots, dozens, all the way through New Jersey," the driver answered.

"Lots, that's too bad. What's your name?" he asked the driver.

"Campbell, Tyler Campbell. Why?"

"Well, Mr. Campbell, it doesn't matter to me how many stops there are between here and Farmingdale because you're going to make sure these three get there. Understand?"

"I'll try to remind them to get off at that stop."

"Don't *try*. *Do* it," the officer barked. "Remember, Mr. Campbell, you're in charge of getting them there safe."

The officer turned and stepped off the bus. He was walking along the outside of the vehicle as I walked down the aisle. He stopped at the back, right where Twilight and Sam were sitting, and tapped his nightstick on the glass. We all stared at him. He looked mean and serious, but then his face dissolved into a smile and he walked away.

"What was *that* all about?" Twilight asked.

"I guess he just wanted to make sure we got on the bus okay," Sam answered.

"He was way too interested. It makes me nervous," I added.

"Everything makes you nervous, Alex," Twilight said.

"Did he look familiar to you?" Sam asked.

"Sam, everybody looks familiar to you," Twilight said.

"Not everybody," Sam said.

"He was just a cop making sure three kids got on a bus. That's all. Both of you quit worrying," Twilight told us. "We're practically home free. Just sit back, relax and we'll be home before you know it."

I sat, but there was no way I was going to relax quite yet. There was something that kept niggling inside of me. Why was that cop so interested in us? Why did he ask our names?

I kept an eye on the front of the bus and watched as another dozen passengers boarded the bus. On schedule, the big bus door closed and it pulled away from the terminal. Just as it turned the corner, I caught sight of the officer. He'd been standing just out of our sight, watching the bus. My nervous feeling got more nervous.

As the city started to fade away I began to feel as though a weight were lifting off my shoulders and chest. In just over an hour we'd be safely back in Farmingdale. We decided to use the time to get our stories straight, because we knew our parents would ask us a lot of questions. We agreed on a bunch of things—Twilight's father was nice, but flaky; we went to the Statue of Liberty, the toy store and the concert; and we mainly ate junk food. It was best to stick to the truth as much as possible. I once heard somebody say that the best lie was telling half the truth, and really, everything we were going to say was the truth. Except for the little part about Twilight's father being there. And according to Twilight he really was a flake, and nice.

Twilight had wanted to add one more fact—that he'd invited us back again in a few months—but there was no way I'd agree to that.

We took turns quizzing each other. Twilight was great! By the time she was finished telling us what had happened, I almost believed she was telling the truth. I wasn't nearly as good, but I did okay. Sam, on the other hand, was pathetic.

"Sam, you should just try to stay quiet and not say much," Twilight suggested.

"I can convince people of what happened!" he protested.

"Sam, believe me, I know acting. And you just don't have it. Stick to being a genius," Twilight said.

"Besides, we don't have time to argue about it, we've got to make our move now," I interrupted.

"Move?" Sam asked.

"We don't want to get off the bus in the middle of town. Somebody could see us. We want to get off where we got on," I explained.

Twilight grabbed her bag and started up the aisle. Sam and I swam up the aisle after her, pulling on each seat in succession until we reached the driver.

"Can you let us off up ahead?" Twilight asked.

He turned to Twilight. "The regular stop is in town. I'm not allowed to let people off on the highway."

"But we got picked up on the highway!" she protested.

"Pickups and drop-offs are different things."

"Come on, it means we'll have to walk all the way back to our houses. Please!" she begged.

"No can do. We'll be there in less than two minutes—just hold your horses."

Sam pushed Twilight aside. "I don't know about holding my horses, but I don't think I can hold my breakfast," he moaned.

"What?" The driver was obviously not happy to hear that.

"My breakfast, my *big* breakfast . . . three eggs and ham and . . . uhhhhh . . . I'm feeling bus-sick . . . I think I'm going to throw up."

"It'll be okay, kid—hold on for just two more minutes!" the driver pleaded.

"I can't," Sam replied as he leaned right over the driver.

"Give me a break, kid. I'm the one who has to clean up the bus at the end of my run!"

"Can't wait." Sam gagged. He clutched one hand over his mouth and doubled over, his face practically in the driver's face.

"Okay, okay!" the driver yelled.

I grabbed on to the seat as the bus abruptly slowed down and swerved onto the soft shoulder. The driver brought the bus to a stop and the door popped open.

"Hurry, get off!" he ordered Sam.

Sam jumped through the door and Twilight and I quickly followed him onto the gravel shoulder. Sam was all doubled over.

"Are you okay, Sam?" Twilight asked.

Sam straightened up. "Okay? Am I okay? I'm *better* than okay, I'm fantastic. And you two didn't think I could act!" And with that he turned and walked away.

Twilight and I stood there with our mouths hanging open. By the time we recovered, he'd walked behind the bus and started to cross the highway. We ran after him. The engine revved up and the bus started off. Twilight blew him a kiss and the three of us ran off into the ravine.

Walking through the ravine, we went over our story one last time. I caught sight of the school and felt a real sense of relief.

"What's with the smile?" Twilight asked.

I tried to wipe it off my face but it resurfaced. "I'm just happy to be home."

"Me too!" Sam agreed.

"It was pretty cool. You never thought we'd get away with it, did you, Alex?"

"Nope," I admitted. "I didn't think we had a chance."

We came to Twilight's street first. We stopped at her front path.

"Well, guys, I guess this is it. I'll call you both later on tonight. Thanks for a great weekend," she said.

"Yeah, call me tonight," I said.

Twilight bounded up her front walk and we started off for Sam's place. We were about halfway down her street when we heard a shout.

"Wait!" We turned around to see Twilight running after us. My stomach dropped.

"What's wrong?" I asked.

"Read this!" she said as she thrust a piece of paper into my hands.

"'Dear Twilight,'" I read out loud. "'I'm at the Sterlings'. Mrs. Sterling suggested that we all get together—along with Alex's parents—for a little lunch so we can get to know each other better. Love, Mom.'"

"This isn't good," I said. "Not good at all."

"Don't freak out," Twilight said. "We're just going to have a meal together. Stick to our story and we'll be okay. There's nothing to worry about."

"Are you sure?"

"If they knew what we'd done, do you really think they'd be throwing us a party?" she asked.

That made sense.

As we walked toward Sam's house, I saw my mother's car sitting in the driveway. I felt as if my legs were made of lead and I had to drag them the last block and a half. Sam opened the door and walked in. Our parents came out of the living room and greeted us with hugs and kisses before ushering us into the living room. I sat down on the couch between my parents. For the first time in days I felt as though I could close my eyes and still be safe.

"So, son," Sam's dad asked, "did you enjoy your weekend?"

Sam blurted out our whole story in one burst. I just felt relieved that he had told it all correctly.

"Weren't you afraid, being there in the city?" my mother asked.

Before I could answer my father started to speak.

"The city is a pretty dangerous place full of dangerous things and dangerous people. Thank goodness you three weren't *alone in the city*. Now that would be scary, don't you agree, Alex?"

"Uh, yeah, Dad, sure . . . the city is scary, I guess . . . but it's not like I was by myself."

Sam's father turned to Sam again. "What was your favorite part of the weekend?"

"That's easy. The Garden."

"The concert was pretty good," I said, jumping in before Sam could say anything more.

"And what did your father think of the concert?" Twilight's mother asked.

Twilight gave her a confused look. "Since when do you care what he thinks about anything?"

"I was just curious," she said. "Did he have any complaints?"

"Not a one. He didn't complain about anything that happened all weekend," Twilight said. She turned to me and gave me a little wink. This wasn't going well. I had to get away from there.

"Can we go home? I'm not feeling well," I announced, borrowing the line that had worked so nicely for Sam.

Suddenly Mr. Sterling got up. There was a look of panic on his face. "Quiet, everybody, quiet!"

The room went still.

"Did you hear that?" he asked in a whisper.

There was total silence, and then we could hear sounds coming from behind the kitchen door.

"There!" Mr. Sterling said. "Did you hear it?"

The hairs on the back of my neck stood on end. Mr. Sterling slowly moved to the kitchen on tiptoe. He grabbed the doorknob and flung the door open. In an explosion of fury, three large men came charging through!

"WHERE ARE THOSE KIDS?" one of them yelled.

I thought my heart was going to jump right out of my chest! They'd followed us here! And we were dead!

Chapter Sixteen

Just when I thought I was going to die, the big guys stopped. It all got a little confusing after that. I looked up at my father, and he was wearing a big smirk on his face. My mother had her hand over her mouth—I wasn't sure what she was thinking. And then out of the kitchen walked Mrs. Watson, our school secretary, and she looked mad . . . really mad!

"I see you've had a chance to meet my boys," Mrs. Watson said. "You led them on a merry chase down in New York last night."

"These . . . these . . . are yours?" Twilight asked, incredulous, waving her arms around the room.

"Yep, my boys," Mrs. Watson answered. "Although I

should have disowned 'em for not being able to find the three of you." All of her boys looked away from their mother. "But I guess these three shouldn't get all the blame—apparently the other four are no better."

"I thought they looked familiar," Sam noted absently.

"Did you kids really think you could get away with this charade?" Twilight's mother demanded angrily.

"We thought we had a chance," Twilight answered. "How did you find out?"

"Your father called yesterday evening, asking to speak to you."

"I guess I didn't think about that possibility," Twilight confessed.

"I guess you didn't think of *any* possibilities. You three could have gotten yourselves in big trouble!"

"Could have, but we didn't. We're fine!" Twilight protested.

"Yeah, we got away from that gang," Sam added.

"Gang? What gang?" Sam's mother asked. All the mothers suddenly looked even more worried.

"It wasn't really a gang. Just some kids, that's all," Twilight said, trying desperately to backpedal.

"Are you sure they weren't a gang?" Sam asked her.

"*Positive*," Twilight hissed.

"And then, after I spoke to your father, I called Alex's parents and Sam's parents. You can imagine how worried *they* were! I told them that you were probably staying at

Brice's apartment. Where *did* you stay?" Twilight's mother asked.

"Brice's apartment ... the first night," Twilight answered.

"But not the second night?" her mother said. "Why not?"

"We saw *them* waiting for us," Twilight answered, pointing to the Watson boys.

"You let them see you!" Mrs. Watson barked at her sons. She reached out and slapped the closest one across the top of his head.

"Sorry, Mom," he mumbled under his breath.

"Where did you sleep, then?" Mr. Sterling asked.

"A car, a Volvo," Sam answered. "You know, Volvo has a very good safety rating," he added helpfully.

"Good gracious, a car! What were you three thinking of? Or were you even thinking at all? Can you even imagine what might have happened to you?" My father was furious. "And you must have realized that you'd get caught sooner or later."

"We were really hoping for later ... much later," I answered, and instantly regretted my reply.

"I'm glad you still have your sense of humor, Alex. We didn't think it was funny! We were worried to death until that policeman called and told us he'd put you on the bus this morning," my mother said.

"The policeman!" Twilight exclaimed.

"I knew something was funny from the way he was talking to us. But why didn't he pick us up?" I asked.

"He was doing me a favor. He works out of my police division," one of the Watson boys replied. "I had officers checking out places like the bus station. One of the restroom attendants told him he talked to two runaways. After he made sure you got on the bus, he called me."

"It's time for us to get home," my mother said as she rose from her seat.

"Us too," Twilight's mother agreed.

Twilight turned to me. "I'll give you a call when I—"

"Don't count on it," her mother interrupted. "You won't be talking to anybody for a long time."

"But, Mom!" Twilight objected.

Her mother fixed her with a deadly gaze and Twilight buttoned it. I left, trailing behind my parents, without saying another word. We were caught, but at least we were home.

It had been two weeks since that fateful meeting at Sam's house. All of the parents had agreed we'd be grounded, except for school, for three weeks. For the first two weeks of that time we weren't even allowed to talk to each other. That was really hard at school, where we could see each other but weren't allowed to exchange words. It seemed as if Mrs. Ready or Mr.

Roberts or Mrs. Watson was always standing over us, watching, waiting for us to even try to talk.

One of the strangest things, though, was how Mrs. Watson treated me. She still scowled at me, but a couple of times she came over and for no reason ruffled my hair and made a joke. At first that didn't make any sense to me. Why would she like me more for getting into the biggest trouble of my life? Then I realized that me getting into major trouble probably reminded her of her own boys.

Thanks to Twilight, the other kids heard all about what happened. At first that really bothered me. It was bad enough doing something stupid, and worse getting caught, but somehow everybody thought it was "way cool." Apparently, the way Twilight was telling the story, I was a hero who bravely took on the gang leader instead of sort of stumbling into him and bumping my head.

At noon on Sunday the two-week period of silence would be officially over. The digital clock on my night table read eleven fifty-nine and fifty seconds. I picked up the phone and pushed in the seven numbers as I counted down the last few seconds. The phone gave just the first buzz of a ring before it was picked up.

"Hi, Alex," Sam said, before I'd even had a chance to say hello.

"Hi, Sam . . . good to talk to you."

"Can you hold on for a second?"

"Yeah, I guess . . ." I replied, although I was a bit confused. We don't talk for two weeks and he puts me on hold? The line went silent, and I thought about what an incredibly long and hard fourteen days it had been. Aside from dealing with my parents' being so disappointed in me, the worst part was just being out of touch with Sam. I hadn't gone more than ten hours without talking to Sam in years.

There was also one other thought troubling me. During the past two weeks I'd watched Twilight talking and laughing with other kids at lunch and recess. I had to admit to myself that I was worried that Twilight would find them more interesting than Sam or me, and when the grounding was up she wouldn't want to spend time with us any more. The only thing worse than getting involved in another one of her plans would be *not* getting involved.

The phone came back to life.

"Hi, Alex, sorry to keep you waiting," Sam apologized.

"That's okay, it's good just to hear your voice."

"Yours too. By the way, say hello to Twilight."

"Hi, Alex!" Twilight chimed in.

"Twilight! What are you doing at Sam's?"

"I'm not . . . I'm at home," she answered.

"But how . . . ?"

"I arranged it, Alex. I used a special kit to convert my phone to make conference calls," Sam explained. "After all, I've been in my room a lot the past two weeks. I had to do something to pass the time."

I smiled broadly. "Sam, you are amazing."

"Thank you, Alex. You're right, I *am* amazing."

"So, what have you two guys been up to while I've been missing you both so much?" Twilight asked sweetly.

My smile grew even wider. She'd been missing us . . . missing *me*. "Not much, Twilight, just reading."

"And you, Sam?" she prompted.

"Oh, mainly thinking."

"Thinking? Thinking about what?" Twilight asked.

"Well, I've got an idea . . ."